Ten feet away and moving directly toward us was a tall boy carrying a knapsack. He wore a leather jacket, jeans, and a pair of high tops. His hair was perfectly cut and combed. He had blue-gray eyes, thick eyelashes . . . the works. His dimples and square jaw made me think of a movie star. And to everyone at Jordan Junior High, he might as well have been.

His name was Travis McAllister.

Coolest of the cool. Primo person. Star basketball player.

EJ's whole body wagged, as if he knew who Travis McAllister was and that his owner should have a chance to meet this guy. But whatever EJ thought, it was definitely bad timing. When I'd looked in the mirror before breakfast, I could have been declared a disaster zone. I panicked.

What if he talks to me? What'll I say?

"Nice dog," Travis said. "What's his name?" He scratched EJ behind the ears.

"EJ," I choked out a faint whisper. My mouth had gone dry from hanging open for too long.

1

DARCY's
GREAT EXPECTATIONS

Joni Eareckson Tada
and Steve Jensen

Chariot Books™
A Division of Cook Communications

Chariot Books™ is an imprint of David C. Cook Publishing Co.
David C. Cook Publishing Co., Elgin, Illinois 60120
David C. Cook Publishing Co., Weston, Ontario
Nova Distribution Ltd., Eastbourne, England

DARCY'S GREAT EXPECTATIONS
© 1994 by Joni Eareckson Tada and Steve Jensen

All Scripture quotations are taken from *The Living Bible*© 1971, owned by assignment by the Illinois Regional Bank N.A. (as trustee). Used by permission of Tyndale House Publishers Inc., Wheaton, IL 60189. All rights reserved.

Cover design by Elizabeth Thompson
Cover illustration by Chris Dall
First Printing, 1994
Printed in the United States of America
98 97 96 95 94   5 4 3 2 1

CIP applied for/LC number

Read all the books in the Darcy series

For Joy Kragenbrink,
who reminds me a lot of Darcy

1

"Remember, Darcy, stick close to the machine. It's an old copier and doesn't always stop at the number you want," Miss Graf told me. "When you're finished, write down the number of copies you made and my name on this sheet of paper. That way the people in the office will know how many copies our department has made."

Miss Graf is the head floor nurse at Park Memorial Hospital where I volunteer as a candy striper in the afternoons. Miss Graf's white uniform is always spotless, her shoes clean as a whistle, and her face clear and smooth. If it weren't for her harsh and crackly voice, you'd think she was the youngest nurse in the hospital. She isn't. And she isn't the easiest to please, either.

"No problem!" I announced eagerly. It was my second week as a candy striper and I was trying hard to satisfy everyone.

Candy stripers are volunteers who help the nurses

in lots of different ways. We're called candy stripers because of our pink-and-white-striped shirts. We don't get paid anything, but it's okay. I just want to help out. I come in after school or on weekends as often as I like.

I was a particularly eager candy striper because I wanted a chance to do the kinds of jobs I thought a real nurse's helper should do: taking temperatures, changing bandages, helping patients in therapy. Up until now, my hours had been filled with wiping counters, delivering mail, and sorting papers. *Maybe tomorrow*, I said to myself at the end of each day. But tomorrow never changed. I was still doing boring jobs like copying memos for doctors who would probably toss them in the trash anyway.

"You want seventy-five copies, right?" I asked.

"Right," Miss Graf answered. "I'll see you later. Put the finished copies on my desk." She left the copy room and closed the door behind her.

I turned back to the machine and keyed in my request for seventy-five copies.

"Push 'start,'" I told myself out loud.

The machine groaned at first, then shot out blue-green rays of light that leaked from under its cover. I began my count, knowing the machine might goof up as Miss Graf had said and not stop at seventy-five.

Whoosh, thwack! One.

Whoosh, thwack! Two.

Whoosh, thwack! Three.

The copier spit out the copies in a loud, rapid rhythm. The sound filled the small room. It hurt my ears, so I held my hands over them.

Whoosh, thwack! Eight.

Whoosh, thwack! Nine.

The loud sound and the small room started to get to me. I felt hot and my face turned red. My counting of the copies seemed more like a count-down to an explosion. *I've got to get out of here!*

I didn't give myself a chance to find any other solution.

I'll just leave the room and count while I'm in the hallway. Then when it's about done, I'll come back in and turn it off.

Without missing a beat—*thirteen, fourteen, fifteen*—I wheeled out of the room and shut the door behind me. The sound of the machine quieted to a pleasant echo. I felt relieved and continued the count in my head. *Eighteen, nineteen, twenty.*

Feeling good about my decision, I relaxed in my chair and looked around me. The empty hall stretched a long way in both directions. Flickers of blue, green, and red reflected off the shiny floor from rooms where patients were watching TV. It was three-thirty on a Monday afternoon, time for day nurses and night nurses to meet so that the new shift could be told what had happened during the day.

"Twenty-five, twenty-six, twenty-seven," I whispered out loud.

Directly opposite me was a large window looking out on the hospital courtyard. Only I couldn't see outside. The day was dark and cloudy, so the window showed the trees and bushes only partially.

The rest of the image was a reflection of me with my back to the copy room door. In the glaring light of the hallway I looked like a ghost. You couldn't make out my features, just the image of a twelve-year-old girl with light brown hair, sitting in a wheelchair. *Thirty-eight, thirty-nine, forty* . . .

I moved closer to the window and squinted at my reflection the way I did each morning in the mirror.

I haven't grown one bit, I thought.

Turning my face left and then right, I saw the same stupid freckles, limp brown hair with frazzled ends, a couple of pimples here and there, and a frumpy uniform. There seemed to be no shape to me, what with my lower half being cut off by the window ledge and wall. The upper part of my body just sat in a heap. I straightened up, threw my shoulders back, and scolded myself for slouching. *Forty-six, forty-seven, forty-eight* . . .

The wheelchair is a natural part of me, and I took no notice of it. It's been part of my life for the last five years, since I was hit by a car that paralyzed me from the waist down. I'm a paraplegic—that means I can't move my legs.

I frowned as I finished my self-inspection. I wheeled closer to the window, leaned on the ledge, and cupped my hands around my face so I could stare outside. It was a boring January afternoon. Gray all over, with no hint of a break in the clouds or sun. *Fifty-one, fifty-two, fifty-three* . . . I continued counting to the quiet beat behind me.

Snow lay on the ground like a dirty gray carpet,

splotched with black near the edge of the road where cars had sprayed dirt and water. The streets were empty. Nothing moved except for the flash of blinkers from a van parked across the way. *Fifty-seven, fifty-eight, fifty-nine . . .*

I stared at the van and began to imagine a story. *Some guy is here to elope with his fiancée. His friends blocked off the street at both ends. He's inside the apartment building now, and he's carrying his sweetheart in his arms.*

"Are you sure we should get married, Michael?" she says.

"Of course, my dear. Your father refuses to let us get married, but I've worked hard for you and no one can stop us now."

The hero descends the stairs to take her to the van. Just ten steps and he'll make it down the stairs. Ten, nine, eight, seven, six, . . .

I jumped, realizing that I was daydreaming. The copies! *Sixty-seven, sixty-eight . . .* I turned and scooted back to the copy room. The sound of the machine grew louder as I approached.

I turned the handle of the door to the left, but it didn't move. I jerked it to the right. Locked! The muffled *whoosh-thwack, whoosh-thwack* of the machine continued, as did my counting. *Seventy, seventy-one, seventy-two . . .* I felt a wave of panic, immediately followed by a wave of guilt.

Remember, Darcy, stick close to the machine. I heard Miss Graf's voice in my head. I had remembered, but I hadn't listened.

I shut my eyes tightly, hoping that maybe this

time the machine would be kind and stop on its own at seventy-five. Maybe they'd fixed it and Miss Graf didn't know. *Seventy-four, seventy-five, seventy-six . . .*

Maybe I counted wrong. I started back at sixty-five again. *Oh, please!*

The machine kept right on grinding away while I counted another ten copies. The *whoosh-thwacking* was still going strong.

My shoulders sank. *What do I do now?* I wrestled with the door handle again, while the machine inside seemed to get louder and faster. I pictured it turning into a monster, laughing at its freedom to destroy my life!

I was embarrassed about not following instructions. And I was worried about what I would fill out on the form—the form that would be used to charge the nursing department. Would they make me pay for the copies? I was afraid to ask, but I knew I had to tell someone. Miss Graf was at the end of the hall in the meeting with the nurses coming on duty. I took off in that direction. I didn't really rush, because I needed time to think. How would I explain what happened? What excuse could I give? As hard as I thought, I could find no answer that would keep me out of trouble.

The nurses were crowded around the counter of the nurses' station. Some stood out in the hallway, others were sitting behind the counter. Miss Graf sat at the desk giving instructions.

"Mrs. Matthews in Room 404 has been complaining a lot. Be firm with her, but remember she just came out of surgery yesterday. Mr. Jones in 411 just had his medication increased."

"Uh, Miss Graf," I interrupted.

She didn't hear me.

"Miss Graf," I called out a little louder.

She looked up over her glasses. "Not now, Darcy. I've got to finish this meeting. Later, okay?"

I should have said no, but I couldn't get the word out. Instead I sat back in my chair and stared at the clock overhead. I didn't really want to tell her about the machine. And besides, I figured, if things got really bad, it would be partially her fault for making me wait.

I lost count of how many copies were being churned out. It had to be in the hundreds by now, maybe in the thousands!

It was at least five minutes before the meeting ended. Nurses left and headed toward their posts. Several greeted me politely. I smiled back, but my heart was pounding.

"Miss Graf?" I asked.

"Yes, Darcy, what is it?" She had a schedule spread out on the desk in front of her, and she didn't look up. "Did you finish the copies?"

"Well, yes, but . . ."

"Then lay them on my desk here. I'll get to them later. Now head down to the X-ray lab and pick up the latest files for me. You know the routine." She was totally preoccupied with the stuff on her desk.

By now the count in my head had reached at least seventeen million. I knew the machine had to be stopped. I finally said it as best I could. "Yes, but you see, the door locked behind me, and I left the copies in there and—"

"That's no problem. I'll get them on my way down the hall."

She'd missed the point. I was forced to say it again, this time with more panic in my voice.

"But there is a problem. You see, I left the room while the machine was still copying, and—"

I didn't need to explain any more. Without looking my way, Miss Graf grabbed her keys from a drawer and sped down the hall. I followed quickly and quietly, dreading her reaction. My days as a candy striper seemed numbered.

Miss Graf had taken a risk in letting me volunteer in the first place. A few supervisors wondered about my ability to squeeze my wheelchair safely around the equipment and the beds. One even thought I'd make people feel worse. "She's in a wheelchair. She'll depress people who are trying to get better." These were the thoughts that haunted me as I caught up to Miss Graf.

She flung the door open. The copy room was a disaster zone. There was paper everywhere. Little piles littered the entire floor and some sheets had even slipped under the door and out into the hallway. Some paper had managed to climb back up on top of the machine.

Miss Graf stood over the machine and stared at the count indicator: 483! The room was silent except for one last sputter from the motor. It was as if it breathed a sigh of relief after copying for so long.

"I told you to stick by the machine!" Miss Graf shouted.

I hung my head. "I'm sorry." Tears filled my eyes and hovered on the rim.

Miss Graf saw how upset I was and quickly changed her tone of voice. "Oh, come on now. Don't cry." She tried to sound nice as she gathered papers off the top of the machine. "I should have let you stop the meeting to tell me. Besides, maybe now they'll see why we need a new copy machine."

She said some other things to cheer me up, but I could tell that underneath she was still mad. She knew it, too, and gave up the nice tone of voice.

"Next time, Darcy, please do what you're told! You'll never be a good candy striper if you don't stick to your job. You'll never be good at anything if you don't follow orders. Now clean up this mess!"

I said a soft "Yes, ma'am" and bent over to pick up the papers around my chair.

"Don't forget to keep out seventy-five copies— all facing the same direction. Place them on my desk. The rest you can put in the recycling bin. And put your name underneath mine on the form!"

She left the room without looking at me, mumbling something I didn't understand about budgets and expenses.

I glared at the copier as if it were my younger brother, Josh. "You stupid machine," I grumbled. I set about picking up the rest of the paper. At one point I giggled at the mess I had made. If only my friends could see me now. Darcy the Duplicator. Darcy the Crazed Copier.

One thing encouraged me. "Next time," Miss Graf had said. "Next time" meant that I would be allowed to stick around longer. I would be given another chance.

I did as Miss Graf told me and cleaned up the room. Then I stacked seventy-five copies in proper order, placed them on my lap, and wheeled down to the nurses' station, where I laid the copies on the counter. The clock said four-fifteen. My mom was due to pick me up in front of the hospital in half an hour, but since there were no nurses or doctors in sight, I decided to hang out by the nurses' station. I picked up a magazine off the counter and flipped through it, waiting patiently and hoping to stay out of trouble until Mom came.

The magazine was boring. My eyes scanned the nurses' station. There were papers, files, phones, a potted plant, bottles of medicine, a cup of coffee—all signs of busy people having been there. Then I saw it. A flashing yellow light on a board next to the phone. It was the board that alerted the nurses when a patient needed help. I moved closer to see who had the call button on. 413, the number read. Mrs. Hamlin's room.

I waited for someone to show up, but no one came. The light kept flashing. I pictured the worst. Maybe Mrs. Hamlin had fallen out of bed. Maybe her medicine tube was twisted. Maybe her heart had stopped!

I thought of the copy room disaster. That had happened because I'd decided to do something on my own. I was now faced with the same kind of problem. It wasn't my job to go to patients when they pushed the button. *What if I do something really dumb again and get in big trouble?* I hoped Mrs. Hamlin would give up. But the longer the light flashed, the more I worried.

Finally my fear of what might happen if I didn't do something won out. I tossed the magazine back on the counter and made my way down to 413. Upon entering the room, I saw Mrs. Hamlin lying in bed, trying to reach for something on her tray table. I moved quietly, curious about what she was trying to do. She saw me out of the corner of her eye as I reached her bed.

"Well, hello, Darcy," she said with a weak smile.

I was relieved. At least she wasn't dying.

"Thank you for coming down. It isn't an emergency—I just wanted someone to reach my Bible for me."

I glanced back at the tray table. There at the farthest end was a worn olive-green Bible. Its edges were frayed, and brown tape held the binding together. It felt even older than it looked as I picked it up to hand to her. I thought it would fall apart in my hands.

"Thank you, dear," she said. Her hands shook as she opened the Bible. She tried to lift her head up to see better but it was too hard for her. Her head fell back against the pillow, and she laid the Bible on her chest.

"It seems I'm just too weak, Darcy, to read my Bible. Thank you anyway." She closed her eyes.

"I can read for you," I said. "I enjoy reading the

Bible. I've got one at home."

"Oh, would you? Are you sure you have time? You're not too busy?"

"No. I've got until four forty-five before my mom comes. I finished all my other jobs," I said. "Besides, I'm in the way sometimes. Hiding here with you would be great."

My last comment didn't escape her notice.

"Hiding?" she said as she opened her eyes and stared straight into mine. "Want to tell me about it?"

Ordinarily I would have said no, but the sting of being scolded by Miss Graf and my anger at being given boring jobs made me spill out everything about the copy room disaster.

"It's not fair," I said when I finished. I was almost whining. "I really want to help people, but all I get to do is deliver forms, paper clip stuff together, tack things on bulletin boards, and clean up after the nurses' coffee breaks. I feel more like a maid than a nurse's helper."

Mrs. Hamlin didn't scold me, but she didn't try to comfort me either. She just listened carefully and held my hand in hers.

"Darcy?" she finally asked.

"Yes?"

"Will you read to me now?"

It seemed as if she hadn't even heard me share my problem. But that was okay. I obeyed her anyway.

"Read I Corinthians 13," she requested. "I like that chapter. For some reason it comforts me."

The pages of the Bible were as worn as its cover. Notes in small handwriting were all over the top and bottom margins of each page. Some pages had gray smudge marks. Some had holes where ink had seeped through the pages as though they were paper towels.

I found the chapter easily enough. It must have been her favorite—the page was almost a blur of ink and smudges with underlining everywhere.

I cleared my throat and read as best I could. "Love is very patient and kind, never jealous or envious, never boastful or proud."

"Isn't that peaceful?" Mrs. Hamlin interrupted. "I think of Jesus every time I hear those words."

"Yeah," I nodded, though I hadn't actually thought of it that way before. I lifted the Bible closer to my eyes and read on. "It does not hold grudges and will hardly even notice when others do it wrong. If you love someone you will be loyal to him no matter what the cost. You will always believe in him, always expect the best of him and always stand your guard in defending him."

I saw then why Mrs. Hamlin had me read this particular chapter. Especially the part about not holding grudges and hardly even noticing when others do you wrong. I expected a lecture. Instead, Mrs. Hamlin said something quite different.

"You know, Darcy, those verses are about you. I think you're patient and kind and loyal. You're certainly kind to me, and you stay by me whenever I need you. It's not your job, after all, to answer the nurse call button. But you did."

"But what about those awful things I said about working here?" I asked. "I didn't feel loving then."

"We all can feel that way at times. But remember that who we are deep down is what really counts. It's obvious you love God. You just need to let Him teach you how to love people in a deep-down way. Do your job well. Stick to it. And stick by your friends. That's what Jesus would do."

"Yeah," I nodded. "I guess so."

The room became quiet again. The twilight from her window made the ceiling glow in a warm, soft color. Music from somebody's radio down the hall drifted into the room. It was very peaceful, but Mrs. Hamlin was too tired to talk.

Her surgery must have been hard, I thought as I leaned over to pull up her covers a bit. Her hair, pinned up in a bun on the day she arrived, now lay on her pillow, spread out like a fan. It was mixed with browns and grays. The brown streaks were as lively and bright as a teenager's. The gray wisps looked cold and stiff. The surgery and illness had left her pale except for two rosy spots on her cheeks. She breathed slowly and peacefully.

A familiar voice calling my name startled me. It was my mother looking for me. I glanced at my watch and gasped to see how much time had slipped by. It was now five minutes to five.

I carefully placed the olive-green Bible on the bed so it would be within reach if Mrs. Hamlin woke up. I took one last look at her as though I were a real nurse checking to see if things were okay, and then turned to wheel away.

" 'Bye," I whispered.

It was not until I was near the door that I heard a faint reply.

"Good-bye, Darcy."

2

I forgot about the quiet of Mrs. Hamlin's room as I sat in the lobby of Jordan Junior High the next morning. Hundreds of kids poured out of yellow buses and minivans in a steady stream of noise and jostling. I had parked myself against the brick wall so as not to trip anybody.

What a crazy place. I sighed as I watched kids push and shove. *We're all lined up here waiting to go into a building where we have to sit still for seven hours and avoid as much work and embarrassment as possible. No wonder so many of us don't like it.*

My dog, EJ, stood tall next to me. EJ was a Golden Retriever. His face was always in a smile and his dark brown eyes were cuter than anyone else's, even some of the cutest guys in my classes. Although he wasn't an official service dog, EJ did things for me like pick up my books and reach for stuff in my backpack. Mr. Sandstrom, the principal of Jordan, let me bring him to school. Some parents got angry about that, but most people liked the idea. Even the teachers liked having EJ march into the classroom, looking all serious and dutiful about his job. They said it helped to keep the classroom quieter.

There wasn't a kid in school who could resist greeting EJ each morning as they walked by in the lobby. Some kids would lean down to press their faces against his or ruffle his ears. One or two kids even brought dog treats for him. I didn't allow people to distract him during the rest of the day, so I made certain he got plenty of attention before school started. EJ rewarded each greeting and pat with a wag of his tail or a lick on the hand.

Though I didn't want to admit it, I relished the attention EJ attracted. It felt good owning a dog that kids liked, and I sensed that some kids were jealous of me. I had to fight off feeling smug about that. Being paralyzed for a long time had made me feel envious of other kids, and now it was their turn. I already had friends—good friends like Mandy, Chip, April, and Kendra—but something inside me wanted more. Owning EJ was a way of getting what I wanted.

I scanned the sea of kids pouring through the front doors and down either hallway to see if Mandy and April had arrived. No sign of them. I was almost ready to move on when EJ started one of his tail-wagging-his-body fits.

"What is it, EJ?" I asked. The lobby was beginning to empty out and I didn't recognize anyone I knew. I followed his gaze. Where it led me took my breath away.

Ten feet away and moving directly toward us was a tall boy carrying a knapsack. He wore a leather jacket, jeans, and a pair of high tops. His hair was perfectly cut and combed. He had blue-gray eyes, thick eyelashes . . . the works. His dimples and square jaw made me think of a movie star. And to everyone at Jordan Junior High, he might as well have been.

His name was Travis McAllister.

Coolest of the cool. Primo person. Star basketball player. He wore the neatest clothes. He was seen in all the right places. And if there was a catchy phrase going around school, you could be sure Travis was the one who had started it. He had all the other kids—boys and girls—doing whatever he wanted. And he was in the eighth grade.

EJ's whole body wagged, as if he knew who Travis McAllister was and that his owner should have a chance to meet this guy. But whatever EJ thought, it was definitely bad timing. When I'd looked in the mirror before breakfast, I could have been declared a disaster zone. I panicked.

Call out the National Guard! My clothes, hair, everything is all wrong. What if he talks to me? What'll I say? Darcy, this is dumb. He's just a kid. He's just—

"Nice dog," Travis said. "What's his name?" He scratched EJ behind the ears.

"EJ," I choked out a faint whisper. My mouth had gone dry from hanging open for too long.

"DJ?" he asked.

"No!" I almost shouted to make up for my whisper. "EJ. He's named after the initials on my wheelchair."

Way to go, DeAngelis. Why in the world would you ever mention the wheelchair to someone like Travis? You have a hard enough time having kids accept you for who you are. How stupid can you be?

"Oh," he said, unimpressed. "Does he go hunting?"

"Uh . . . no. He helps me get around and picks things up. He's kind of like a service dog for disabled people, except he's not official 'cause he has a problem with his hips that keeps him from doing a whole lot. He can't be an official service dog with the hip problem, so he doesn't always work for me. . . ." I rambled on as if there wasn't any off-switch in my mouth.

"Oh." He hooked one thumb in his belt loop and with his other hand scratched EJ under the chin. It seemed he was about to leave.

"Saw you play basketball the other day," I said, hoping I could keep him there longer.

"Uh-huh." He squatted down and rubbed EJ's ears.

"You play middle, right?"

"Center. It's called center," he said without emotion.

My face flushed. *I knew that! Why did I say middle? Oh, Darcy, he thinks you're dumb. Your dog's a wimp because he doesn't hunt, and you're an airhead who doesn't know the difference between middle and center.*

26

"Oh, yeah, dumb me," I said. "You play really well."

"Mmm." He stood up.

There was too much dead air between us, but I didn't know what else to say. EJ had done his best to keep Travis there, but I was stuck. I was afraid that whatever I blurted out would be stupid.

"Dar-cyyyy!" April's squeal from across the lobby saved me.

Travis turned in her direction, and April fastened her eyes on him while she spoke to me. "Who's your friend?"

"This is Travis," I said. "He plays basketball. Remember?"

"Darcy, of *course* I remember. Who could forget that great shot in the final seconds last week, right?" She looked up at Travis with one of her Cheshire cat grins. "You were totally awesome."

April rattled on about every drive to the basket and free throw from the foul line that Travis had made in the game. I was shocked at how much she knew about basketball.

Travis seemed impressed that someone as obviously bubble-headed as April could know so much. But April was no dummy. She was an expert at talking to boys and knew what kept them interested.

But not even April could compete with eighth-grade cheerleaders. Four of them, all wearing the stuff you see on mannequins at The Gap, came bouncing up to us.

"Hey, Travis," one called out. "Aren't those dogs a little young for you?"

April scowled.

"Oh, sorry," the cheerleader huffed. "I meant 'dog.' Didn't realize the other two were seventh-grade girls." She tossed back her long hair and gave us a thin smile.

I squinted in disbelief that anyone could be so rude. April fumed and almost opened her mouth to fight back until she looked up at Travis. He seemed bored already with the conversation and walked away.

"See ya around, EJ," he called over his shoulder. The cheerleaders hiked their books up on their hips and sashayed after him.

"Isn't he the most awesome hunk you ever saw?" April said dreamily when Travis and the cheerleaders were far enough away.

"April!" I said. "Don't be a nitwit. Besides, I don't care what he's like. He's not in the same world as you and me. Just drop any idea you have of making friends with him." I tried to be convincing, but I realized that even I had secret hopes that Travis would look my way the next time he saw me.

"Darcy's right," came a voice from behind us. It was Kendra, my eighth-grade friend who had helped me fit in at school when I first came to Jordan. Kendra was a friend to all—seventh and eighth graders alike.

"I saw you guys gawking," she continued. "That guy thinks he's hot stuff. Having everyone tell him how cool he is doesn't help either. If it weren't for the cheerleaders and basketball, he'd be nowhere."

"But he's so cuuute!" April objected. She was

disappointed that someone as with it as Kendra would write off a person everyone else thought was super cool.

"Trust me," Kendra said. "He doesn't care about others. And he's as dumb as a Tyrannosaurus rex!"

The bell rang, signaling that it was time to get to homeroom. April and I headed down the hall together, while Kendra went in the opposite direction. I wanted to forget everything that had just happened, so I described my afternoon at Park Memorial Hospital to April.

"There was paper coming out of the walls!" I said, telling her about the sea of papers.

April's laughter made the memory of the event seem better.

"And then I went down to Mrs. Hamlin's room. She's a real special lady. She made me feel better just sitting by her bedside. And, oh, check this out!" I reached behind my chair and pulled out my Bible from my backpack. We were right outside of homeroom.

"What are you doing?!" April whispered excitedly. "You can't bring that in here!"

"Why not? It's legal."

"Legal, yeah. But cool, no way. Put it away, Darcy, before somebody sees us."

"Just deal with it, April." I gave her an exasperated look. "C'mon, listen to this."

April glanced up and down the hallway to see if anyone was watching while I read from I Corinthians 13. " 'Love does not demand its own way. It is not irritable or touchy. It does not hold grudges and will hardly even notice when others do it wrong.'

"Is that neat or what? Who would think something so cool would be in this thing?" I said eagerly as I turned my Bible this way and that.

"That's real nice, Darcy, but we have to get to class. And besides, Sunday school was two days ago. Leave the Bible at home, okay? This is school."

"I wonder about you sometimes, April," I said, looking at her in disbelief. I didn't mean to judge her, but I really did wonder. Sometimes she acted like someone who didn't care about God at all.

In typical April fashion, she quickly tried to cover her tracks. "Sorry, Darcy. You know me. Just a motor mouth."

The late bell rang, and April crossed to the other side of the hall to her homeroom. I turned around and went into mine. The words from I Corinthians echoed in my mind.

Love does not demand its own way. . . . The words sounded good, but I could feel the needle on my conscience-meter begin to swing, as if pulled in the other direction by all the seventh-grade things April loved so much. I wondered what Travis would think if he saw me with my Bible.

What did it really mean, anyway? Maybe April was right. This was school, not church.

3

The rest of the week at the hospital was as boring as I'd expected.

After Monday's disaster in the copy room, it seemed I was given the worst jobs on purpose. I spent each afternoon taking down the Christmas decorations that had been left on the bulletin boards and along the railing of the hallways. Each piece of garland stretched for twenty feet, the distance between the patients' rooms. I undid five or six thumbtacks for each length and then piled the plastic garland on my lap, moving on to the next strip. By the time I reached the end of a hallway, the garland was piled high on my lap and dragging on the floor.

The work was not only boring, it hurt my fingernails. Each thumbtack was pressed in deep. My fingers throbbed with pain by the time I finished work on Tuesday. Undoing the garlands on the second floor on Wednesday wasn't much better. It wasn't until Thursday that I finally got the idea of using a penknife to dig out the thumbtacks. Brilliant, Darcy.

Though the knife made the job go more smoothly, it also made me rush. And because I was in such a hurry, I didn't notice when some of the garland I had piled on my lap fell down into the left wheel of my wheelchair. It got stuck in the axle and spokes and there I sat, unable to go forward or back until a janitor got it out for me.

"Big job for a young lady, ain't it?" he said kindly as he cut the pieces of garland.

"Yeah, big job," I said sarcastically. "It takes real brains to clean up after people."

The words came out of my mouth before I realized what I had said and to whom—a janitor who earned his living by cleaning up after people! He didn't look up at me. He kept working his knife deeper and closer to the end of the tangled mess.

"I . . . I'm sorry. I didn't mean that . . ." I stumbled over my words, and my face flushed red with embarrassment.

The janitor stopped his work on my chair and looked up.

"Now don't worry about that. I been working this here job for eighteen years now. I know it don't pay much and I don't wear a fancy uniform, but the way I see it, if I don't clean this joint, ain't nobody can come here. The gov'ment would shut the place down for having too many germs. Yes, ma'am, I'm as important as the doctor." He smiled and gave me a wink.

I smiled back, but somehow the words didn't mean much to me. It was okay for him to think that way, but I figured he had no choice. He obviously wanted to be a janitor and clean up after people. I didn't. All I really wanted was be a candy striper in order to help the patients by doing some real nursing. My lesson with Mrs. Hamlin had been buried with each length of garland I had untacked.

"There you go," the janitor said, as he cut the last piece.

I rolled the wheelchair back and forth to be sure there was no hidden string under the axle. It worked fine.

"Thanks," I mumbled.

"Sure thing. Here, I'll take that pile of Christmas stuff for you. Box is at the other end of the hall, ain't it?"

I was completely finished with my stupid job by the time Mom picked me up that afternoon. Miss Graf would have been proud. And although I was tired, I was relieved.

"How was your day, Darcy?" Mom asked as we drove away from the hospital and into a light flurry of snow. I don't know why, but snow always helps me forget bad stuff and get on with new things. Maybe it's the way it covers all the dirt in the gutters and hides the trash on the sidewalks.

"Okay," I piped up in a brighter tone. I didn't want to whine about the garlands, so I changed the subject. "Mom, could I go to the game tomorrow after school and then go to the hospital a little later?"

"What game is that?" she asked.

"It's the championship game for all the boys' basketball teams at school. It's kind of like a league between the classes. The winner of the championship game gets to play another school. You know, the way they do at Monica's school. It's a big thing."

"You mean an intramural game?"

That was the word I meant. There were a lot of those words to learn once you were in junior high. "Yeah, I guess so. Whatever. Anyway, Chip is on one of the final teams, and I want to go watch with Mandy and the others. May I?"

"I think so. The hospital isn't far from school. If the weather's okay, you can wheel over after the game yourself, all right?"

"Sure. Oh, and can you call the hospital tomorrow for me and let them know?"

"No, Darcy. You can call. I'm not your secretary. If you call as soon as we get home, Miss Graf should still be there."

I didn't argue. I made the call and then sat by the phone and grinned to myself. I had gotten more than permission. I was told that because I had taken down the garlands so quickly, I'd be able to work in the emergency room on Saturday. That made my weekend look great. I'd get to go to the game on Friday, and on Saturday I'd get a chance to do some real nursing!

When the bell rang after my last class on Friday, I hurried to the gym to get a good spot next to the end of the bleachers. A few other kids were also there early and had scrambled up the bleachers to get the best seats. The gym lights cast a blue glow over everything. EJ sat next to me, excitedly watching all the pregame activity.

The pep band warmed up on the sidelines. The scorekeeper tested the buzzer. Cheerleaders lined up along the center of the court, half practicing, half cheering. Some of them weren't comfortable with being in front of people yet, and it showed. They huddled together as if to avoid looking at the audience after each cheer.

Dumb, I thought.

Students and parents began to file into the gym in a steady stream. Friends waved at each other across the court. The top row of the bleachers went to the eighth-grade guys. The seventh-grade guys sat four or five rows below them, content to hit girls on the head or do other stupid stuff to try and get attention.

Dumber yet, I thought.

Mandy, April, and Kendra entered the gym at the far end. I waved. EJ barked and caught Kendra's attention. She pointed in my direction and led the others around the perimeter of the court while EJ wagged his rear end excitedly.

"I'd do the same if I had a tail," I said to EJ. I loved my friends—even April when she teased me.

"Yo, Darcy," April said as she slid up beside me and plopped her coat and books on the floor. "Here to cheer on your hero, Chip?"

I didn't bother to ask what she was talking

about; I knew that would only bring more teasing. I rolled my eyes and looked to Kendra or Mandy for some help in getting out of April's snare. She could be relentless sometimes.

"Lighten up, April," Mandy said as she swung her purse off her shoulder and threw her things on the bench.

I saw some other friends across the way and changed the subject. "There's Jessica and Mrs. Crowhurst. Over here!" I waved.

Jessica is eight years old and has cerebral palsy. She needs lots of love and help, and my friends often spend time with her. Her mom, Mrs. Crowhurst, is our phys ed teacher.

"So how's the princess this afternoon?" I asked Jessica as her mother wheeled her into place beside me. Jessica threw back her head and gave me a big smile. It felt good being a kind of role model for her. I reached over and tousled her hair.

Jessica opened her mouth as if to speak and then looked down at her word board. She pointed to letters of the alphabet on the square piece of wood covered with letters.

"I . . . a . . . m . . . f . . . i . . . n . . . e."

Then she tried to say something with her mouth. Her teeth clenched tight for the first sound, then opened slightly for the second. "Eee . . . ay?" she asked.

"EJ? Oh, he's fine," I answered. "Here, EJ, come over here by Jessica. Up lap, EJ. Lap." I pointed to Jessica's lap. EJ obeyed by getting up on two legs and resting his paws on her lap. He wasn't doing it right, and he knew it. EJ towered over Jessica and looked at me, panting with his tongue hanging out. Jessica buried her head in his soft, furry chest.

"Lap, EJ!" I said sharply. He was supposed to rest his upper body across her legs. He slowly obeyed me, although I could tell he wasn't so sure Jessica's thin legs could handle his 105-pound body. He was twice as heavy as she was.

Jessica didn't mind. She was obviously proud, not only of having the attention of such a beautiful dog, but of sitting with us at the big game.

"Here they come!" Kendra called out. The two teams ran out onto the basketball court and began taking practice shots. Chip's team was in blue at the opposite end of the court. In front of us was none other than the leader of the red team, Travis McAllister. There were cheers and whistles, and a couple of boys on the top row yelled out Travis's name.

"Ooh . . . so that's why we're down here," April said. "Darcy dumped her hero for the dream boat."

I answered in a harsh whisper. "If you don't stop, April, I'll . . . I'll . . ." I was fuming so much I couldn't finish my sentence.

"Yeah, give her a break, April," Mandy chimed in. "You're more interested in boys than any of us. Maybe you're the one who's got a crush on Travis."

April, unlike me, didn't mind the attention. She was more than happy to talk about her feelings. I ignored her and turned my attention to the game.

The warm-ups were finished. The guys threw

the extra basketballs into baskets and sat down on benches on either side of the table where they kept score. The coaches rallied their players as the first string gathered into their own circle.

The announcer tapped the microphone to get everyone's attention. "Let me introduce the players," he shouted.

Applause went up from different sections of the gym as each player was introduced. The players ran out to the center line where they greeted one another and fumbled nervously with their baggy shorts. Chip's name brought the loudest cheering from our end. He looked in our direction when he came onto the court and smiled. He pointed in my direction with his finger, as if he were shooting me.

I shot back. It was one of those "friend" things we often did, and our eyes smiled. Chip and I had been best buddies for a long time. Our families knew each other from way back at church, and we were often at each other's house. In fact, Chip was with me the day I was hit by the car that paralyzed me. It had upset him terribly to see it happen and he struggled with nightmares for a long time afterward. The accident gave us something in common, something only we shared. I knew I could go through hard times with him and he'd always be there. Now that we were getting older, it didn't hurt that Chip was not only a loyal friend but also fun to be around. And I had to admit, he was getting cuter all the time.

Ugh. What a word, cute. I knew almost every girl in the gym was talking about how cute this or that guy was, and I hated it. And here I was thinking the same thing about my friend. I was a little ashamed of myself and mad that when it came down to it, April was probably right: I was here especially to cheer for Chip.

The introduction of Travis's team brought the loudest hooting and hollering, mostly because of Travis. His name was reserved for last. The announcer added an extra oomph to the name, and the gym exploded in cheers and whistles.

Where had I been for six months? I never knew he was such a popular guy. Could Kendra be right? It was hard to imagine that anyone so popular could be as unpleasant as Kendra described.

The buzzer sounded and the game got underway. Both teams started out at a slow, steady pace. Two points at one end, two points at the other. Inbound ball. Dribble down the court. Set up at the top of the key. A fast break, a lay-up, and then the other team got the ball and carried the rhythm.

Chip guarded Travis most of the time. Travis, though the center of the team and assigned to play underneath the basket, wound up with the ball most of the time. He dribbled and shot better than anyone else, so his team was content to let him hog the ball.

Chip wasn't short for his age, but he was no match for Travis. He did manage to steal the ball from him a couple of times. Travis got angry about it, as though Chip had broken some law.

As the game progressed, it was clear the teams were unevenly matched. Chip's guys scored two points for every six of Travis's. I could tell Chip's team was getting frustrated. Their coach changed his strategy after half-time, ordering Chip and another player to double-team Travis.

That meant that for the rest of the game, Travis had two players attempting to block his shot or steal the ball. He handled the pressure well at the beginning, but Chip and his teammate improved as the game wore on. They were able to figure out what Travis was going to do ahead of time, and it irked Travis a lot. He missed several shots and lost the ball often. He looked embarrassed.

Late in the third quarter, the double-team pressure got to Travis. On one occasion, Travis dribbled toward the basket with Chip in front of him, backing up and waving his arms. Chip's teammate was at Travis's side, attempting to slap at the ball. Chip decided to hold his ground and stood to block Travis's path to the basket. Travis lunged ahead, putting his shoulder down and ramming Chip squarely in the chest. Chip flew backward and sprawled on the floor while Travis laid the ball up for an easy shot.

The crowd cheered, but the referee whistled. Everybody quieted quickly.

"Offensive foul on number 33, McAllister. No basket. Blue team's ball!"

Good call! It was obvious that Travis had fouled Chip. Even I knew you weren't allowed to push past a defensive player if he was standing still. But the crowd booed at the referee, anyway, annoyed that their hero had been denied another basket.

The rest of the game went from bad to worse, especially between Travis and Chip. Travis was annoyed by Chip's steady defense, and more than once I saw him shove an elbow into Chip's side. Chip did the best he could to avoid combat.

I felt bad. I also felt like going out on the floor and rolling my wheelchair over Travis's toes. But to tell the truth, I was mad at both players. Travis made me angry because of his rotten attitude. Chip made me angry because he was just taking it.

"Don't be a wimp," I caught myself whispering. Just once I wanted Chip to lash out. "Be tough. Be in charge."

The score at the beginning of the fourth quarter was 63 to 29 in favor of Travis's team. Some kids had already left. A few others were standing up in the bleachers and talking in groups. What a waste.

With just five minutes left to play, I turned to Mandy and the others. "Guys, I gotta go. I told the nurse at the hospital that I'd be there by four. Mandy, would you take EJ back home for me?"

"Sure," she said, reaching for his leash.

"Running out on your hero just because he's losing, Darcy?" April teased.

I clenched my fist, jokingly.

"Just kidding. Have a nice time striping candies!"

" 'Bye, Kendra, Jessica, Mrs. Crowhurst. Take care, EJ," I cooed as I rubbed his head. "You're going home with Mandy, okay?"

EJ licked my face good-bye.

"I'll call you tonight," Mandy yelled to me as I

left, "and let you know how the game ends. And you've got to help me with that algebra assignment."

I answered with a thumbs-up.

I wheeled around the outside of the gym floor and was almost clear of the court when the teams made their way down to my end. I looked up to see Chip dribbling toward me. He passed off to a teammate and then caught my eye. I smiled weakly. It was probably a discouraging thing for Chip to see me leave, but I obviously couldn't explain. I turned my head and wheeled away faster. It wasn't a thing friends should do to each other, but I couldn't think of what else to do.

So Mr. Cool and his zombies play Bakersfield Junior High tomorrow. Congrats, Travis. I hope your hair doesn't get messed up. Wouldn't want those cheerleaders fainting on the floor.

4

I'm usually the first one up on Saturdays. It's a habit from having to get up so early during the school week in order to be ready in time. So even though it was only six forty-five, I was up, dressed, and in place at the table.

There's something about Saturday morning that draws me to our kitchen. I always let breakfast time pass more slowly, cutting my French toast into really small pieces or reading the back of the cereal box including all the stuff about the vitamin daily allowance. It's just a way to delay the start of the day.

While sipping my orange juice, I leaned on my elbow and watched the morning unwind. The sun shone through the white curtains. A winter cardinal perched on the sill, and when I raised up to take a closer look, I noticed a fresh dusting of snow sparkling on the ground. The furnace clicked on and made the kitchen feel warm and cozy.

One by one my family made their entrances into the kitchen. Mom arrived first and got the coffee ready. Then Dad showed up in his Saturday jeans and sweatshirt. Josh came down in a baggy pair of pajamas, his hair sticking out in all directions.

"Want some breakfast before cartoons?" Mom asked him.

"Uh-huh," he said, his eyes half open.

"Scrambled eggs?"

"Uh-huh."

"All I have left are dinosaur eggs. Is that okay?" Mom asked.

"Uh-huh." Josh was still only half awake.

"Two scrambled dinosaur eggs coming up!" Mom said with a laugh. "Honey," she said to my dad, "could you call Monica? She'll need to go to cheerleading practice the same time I drop Darcy off at the hospital."

Dad put down his morning paper and went into the hallway to call upstairs for Monica. When he didn't hear any movement, he went up to knock on her door. Next, the phone rang and Mom answered while she scrambled the eggs.

"Darcy, it's for you. It's Mandy," she said as she handed me the phone.

Good old Mandy. No Saturday morning would be complete without our connecting over the phone.

"Hi," I said, cupping the receiver.

"Hi, Darce. Look, I know you've got plans at the hospital, but do you think you could go to watch the game against Bakersfield today?"

"What time does it start?" I asked.

"Ten-thirty."

I was dying to, but I couldn't. "No, I don't think so."

"You sure? We're all going. Kendra and April, and Chip and the other guys on his team."

I was surprised that Chip would be there. It had been a pretty rough game the day before, and I didn't think he'd want to be anywhere near Travis, let alone cheer for him in a game.

"Chip is going?"

"It's Jordan Junior High's team, right? Why wouldn't Chip go?"

"I don't know. I guess, 'cause . . . never mind. Anyway, I can't go. I've got to work in the emergency room, remember?"

"Emergency?! Hey, I'm sorry you'll miss the game, but that sounds really cool. Do you think you'll see anyone who gets shot or something?"

"Mandy! What a thing to say."

"Just kidding. Well, I gotta get ready. See you tomorrow at church."

"Okay. 'Bye." I hung up the phone with mixed feelings. I always liked goofing off with my friends, but I also knew I had to go to the hospital. It was my big chance to work in the ER (that's nurse talk for emergency room), and I didn't want to miss it.

"Sounds like you turned down an invitation," Mom said as she scooped eggs onto a plate for Josh.

"Yeah," I said as I wheeled back to the table. "It's Jordan against Bakersfield. Travis's team won from our school."

"Travis?"

"Travis McAllister. He's in the eighth grade. I met him the other day in the hall." I acted cool, as if this sort of thing happened all the time.

Dad came down the stairs, with Monica close behind.

"Did I hear the name Travis McAllister?" Monica gushed as she entered the kitchen. "You know Travis McAllister?"

My sister Monica is sixteen years old. Her long hair and pretty face make her one of the popular kids in high school, not to mention the fact that she is just plain nice. Everybody likes her. She knows tons of kids, even those like Travis who don't go to her school. She wasn't about to let me make him sound like no big deal.

"Travis is like the primo kid in the eighth grade. Even some of the kids in our high school know him—I think he got left back a year. Anyway, all the freshmen girls think he's great!"

I shot back at Monica, "Well, Kendra says he's a jerk, and the only ones who think he's cool are air-headed cheerleaders!"

Too late! As the words left my mouth, my eyes caught what Monica was wearing—her cheerleading uniform. I muffled a laugh.

Monica threw Josh's crumpled-up napkin at me and teased, "So, when are you and Travis getting married?"

Rather than continue our friendly fight, Monica poured cereal into her bowl and placed the large box between us.

"Enough gossiping, you two," my mom said. "We've got to get going pretty soon."

"Speaking of going," Dad said, gulping down his last bit of coffee. "I'm supposed to head over to join the work crew at church. Be back around three, I imagine. Thanks for the dinosaur eggs, honey. I'll try to remember to bring home a quart of pterodactyl milk."

That's what I like about Saturday mornings. French toast and cereal, a lot of time, a little teasing, and a whole bunch of laughing.

Except for Josh. My poor little brother was still half awake, stuffing his mouth with breakfast, and the whole thing about dinosaur eggs went right over his head. That made the rest of us laugh all the more.

"Huh?" Josh said as he rubbed his eyes.

I love Saturday mornings.

The hallway heading for the emergency room was a straight shot with a freshly waxed floor. I gave my wheels a hard shove and smoothly coasted in the direction of work. Even from a distance I could tell it would be full of action—alcohol smells, blood and bandages, ambulances, machines, doctors. It would be a little scary, but I knew I could handle it. Nothing was going to upset me.

I pulled to a stop at the desk in the waiting room. The receptionist was all prepared for me and started to tell me my first job. As she fiddled around with things on her desk I thought, *Maybe she's got a stethoscope back there for me . . . or maybe a ther-*

mometer or bandages.

"Take these forms and put them in alphabetical order. Then attach one of these to each form with a paper clip. Got that?"

I stared at her.

"Did you hear me, Darcy?" she asked.

"Yes . . . it's just that, well, is this all?" I wasn't about to hide my disappointment and anger.

"It will take you a good hour, I imagine. When you're done with that, the waiting room needs straightening up. I'll show you what to do later. For now, work on these forms." She plopped the pile of papers on the table in front of me. "Let me know when you're done."

And to think I could have been at the game!

Because I was convinced I should have been allowed to do more important jobs, I had a hard time focusing on the stupid forms. It took me an hour and a half just to finish them. All the while I heard the excitement of ER in the other room. I held on to my disappointment like a dog with a bone.

The receptionist noticed how long it took me. "Hmm. Looks like you did a good job, but it must have been a while since you worked with the alphabet," she teased. "Or maybe I gave you right-handed paper clips instead of left-handed ones." Her attempts to make me smile were not working.

She sighed. "Listen, Darcy. I really appreciate this. These forms make nursing work so hard, and when they're out of order, the doctors go crazy trying to find the information they need quickly. We have to work fast around here."

"Yeah, I guess you're right."

She knew I was disappointed. I went to work in the waiting room, emptying the trash can, putting newspapers back together, dusting the table and chairs. The TV was playing Saturday cartoons and I slowed just a little to watch, curious but a little guilty for looking at something designed for little kids. I aimlessly wiped the rag back and forth across the furniture.

"Candy striper!" one of the nurses called from the next room. I popped my head around the waiting room corner.

The nurse spoke as she ripped off her examining gloves and dug into her pocket for a form, which she quickly handed to me. "We need some syringes from the supply room. Would you please go up and get a box?"

"Sure." Anything to get out of dusting.

I took my time rolling through the hallway to the supply room. "Just another boring day here at Park Memorial," I said out loud to a wall clock.

The clerk at the supply room gave me the box I needed. As I turned to head back to ER, I saw the elevator opposite me let off its passengers. The doors stayed open for a long time, and I stared into the empty chamber. It felt as if the elevator were begging me to enter, saying, "This is my job. Won't someone ride with me? I'm lonely."

It took only a moment to make up my mind. Figuring that the supplies were not all that important and that the ER nurses wouldn't miss me, I accepted the elevator's offer. Within a minute it emptied me at the fourth floor. I turned left down the hall and made my way to Mrs. Hamlin's room.

Mrs. Hamlin was sitting in a chair reading. She looked up at me over her glasses. "Busy day?" she asked.

"Kind of," I lied without thinking.

"Well, come over here and visit with me. It's an honor to have you spend your break time with me."

I didn't tell her it wasn't my break time. I just said thanks and parked myself at the end of the bed, facing her.

"You're feeling better, aren't you?" I said.

"Yes, much better. Thanks to wonderful nurses like you."

"Hah! Nurses like me!"

"Now, Darcy." Mrs. Hamlin had that "teacher tone" in her voice. "Remember what God says about love. Don't forget that that love of yours is supposed to be patient and kind. That's what a nurse is. She's patient with the patients!" She stopped to laugh at her joke.

I laughed a little, too, glad that she was feeling better and truly wanting to please her. But I couldn't hold back my feelings. Mrs. Hamlin just had a way of pulling them out of me.

"I know I'm not supposed to be upset about the jobs I get, but it just doesn't seem fair. They got me all excited about working in ER, but the jobs aren't any different! I'm not one to be patient and kind when it comes to dumb forms."

"But they need you, Darcy. If they didn't need

you, you wouldn't be here. And besides, no matter how they treat you, you've got to find a way to show them love. Find a way, Darcy. Make it creative. Make it fun."

"How?" I asked. "Here I am, an intelligent seventh grader, being sent to pick up syringes from the supply room. How can I make such a simple job fun?"

Mrs. Hamlin lost her soft smile. She looked at me over her glasses and held up her crooked index finger, moving it gently through the air as she spoke. "Darcy, the way of love is first of all loyal. Before it is ever creative or fun, it must be loyal. You have a job to do, it seems. Now go do it!"

I was ready with my argument. "But I love you, too. Aren't I showing loyalty to you by being here?"

"Your love for me, Darcy, is something special, no doubt. I think you love me because I love you. That's nice. But true love will love even when it gets no love in return. And besides, I'm here all day and in no hurry for attention. You can visit me anytime. But those supplies can't wait for just anytime, I suspect."

I gave her my best "hurt puppy" look and slowly left the room. It wasn't how we usually ended conversations, Mrs. Hamlin and I.

I glanced at my watch and hurried back to ER as quickly as I could, afraid and upset about what I had done. But I consoled myself with the thought that the only one feeling bad was me.

The empty waiting area assured me that I was right. At least I hoped so. Only the sound of commotion behind the swinging doors where they treated emergencies gave any sign of people being around. I checked the clock on the wall. A short twelve minutes had passed since I left.

Good. I really haven't been gone that long.

With the box of syringes on my lap, I hit the automatic door button to make my way into the treatment area. Once on the other side of the doors, it was clear something was up. There was a constant motion of people back and forth across the room. There was shouting. A machine bleeped and trays clattered. Doctors and nurses moved like bees around one bed at the other end of the room. I stared and listened.

"Blood pressure eighty over fifty. Pulse fifty-six."

"Get me the adrenaline, stat!"

"Don't lose him, Jerry!"

"Pupils dilated! He's in shock, folks. . . . C'mon, get a move on!"

The activity and the words were strangely familiar, and I fought off a sick stomach. It all reminded me of my day in the ER five years earlier. I remembered people shouting at each other, moving back and forth, yelling out my name to keep me awake. "Darcy, Darcy . . ."

"Darcy!" A nurse broke me out of my daydream. "Where in the world have you been? Give me those syringes now!" She grabbed the box from my lap. "What took you so long? The supply clerk said you left a long time ago. We needed these!" she shouted at me on her way back to the others.

The feeling of guilt crawled up my back and

hung heavy on my shoulders. *What if the person dies because I was late . . . because I didn't do my job?*

An older man dressed in a light blue uniform and a kind of shower cap on his head approached me as I sat there dumbfounded. He looked familiar, but I was too upset to try to place him in my mind. I just hoped he wouldn't chew me out more.

"Darcy," he said, "this is going to be a rough place for a young girl during the next hour. Why don't you head out to the lobby and wait there?"

I didn't want to leave. Staying would make me feel better, and maybe there would be something I could do to make up for my mistake.

"But I've been around something like this before," I pleaded. "I know what it's like. Maybe I can help!"

"I know. I was there the day of your accident, remember? I'm Doctor Vanderhook."

The voice and the face connected in my memory, and I saw that he indeed was my surgeon.

"Doctor Vanderhook!" I exclaimed, relieved to find someone who I knew was my friend. "Oh please, you understand. Please let me stay!"

"Sorry, Darcy. Doctor's orders."

I obeyed his command and wheeled in the opposite direction, weakly pressing the automatic door button. It opened, and I passed slowly to the other side. The doors closed behind me and shut out all the noise. In the sterile quiet, I parked next to the receptionist's desk.

The receptionist was busy filling out forms and answering the phone. I didn't want to talk to her, but just being near her made me feel better. It gave me time to think.

I looked out through the glass doors that opened onto the hospital parking lot. Why hadn't I gone to the game? Why did I ever volunteer? Why couldn't I do at least one thing right?

My view and my thoughts were interrupted by the sight of a woman running frantically toward the building. It seemed she would have broken the glass doors down if they hadn't automatically opened in time.

"Where is he?" she yelled at the receptionist as soon as she got inside. "Where's my son?"

"Your name?" the receptionist asked in an official tone.

"McAllister. Joy McAllister. Where is Travis?"

5

Mrs. McAllister's face was white and her hands were shaking. The receptionist quickly guided her into the emergency room. When the automatic doors opened, the noise and clatter from ER filled the waiting area. I sat and watched them disappear behind the doors. Once again, the waiting area became silent with only the drone of cartoons from the TV.

It was Travis who lay in there at risk, and it was all my fault. What if he died? That would be my fault too. I gave no thought to his accident, whatever it had been, only to my failure to bring the syringes in time. I half expected the doctor or the nurse to walk slump-shouldered through the door any minute, sighing, "We wouldn't have lost him if you hadn't been late with those supplies, Darcy."

Only the sight of our station wagon pulling into the parking lot outside comforted me. My mother parked in the handicap space and signaled for me to come.

"Gotta go. My mom's here," I said to the receptionist who had just returned. Then, before I tripped the glass doors to open, I asked, "Is he going to be all right?"

"Don't know, really. I guess it was a car accident. He seems like a young boy. A little older than you, I think."

"Yeah, he is. I know him from school. He plays basketball."

"Well, he'll be lucky if he can play anything after this. Looked pretty bad to me." The receptionist stopped, seeing how upset I was. She also realized she had told me more than was allowed. "But hey, miracles happen, right?"

I nodded. "See ya." I grabbed my coat off the rack but didn't bother to put it on. I wanted to leave and not hear more than I had to.

On the way home I mentioned the incident to Mom. Thankfully, she could tell I was really upset, and she didn't press me for details. I couldn't have told her anything anyway, since I had no idea how Travis got hurt.

It wasn't until the next day at church that I finally heard the whole story. Chip found me in the hallway outside the worship center and wheeled me back to an empty Sunday school room. He sat down in a chair, and I parked near him. He kept rubbing his knees, wanting to speak but obviously not knowing where to begin.

"You know about Travis?" he finally asked.

"Kind of. I was at the hospital yesterday when they brought him in. But I don't know how it happened, do you?"

Chip was silent for a moment. He swallowed hard and his lip quivered. "Yeah, I know. I was there. Travis got into a fight with a kid from the other team. Jordan beat Bakersfield pretty bad, and this guy was upset with Travis. Seems Travis elbowed him a lot during the game."

"The way he did to you?" I interrupted.

Chip nodded and then went on. "Anyway, the fight looked like it was over with until they got to the end of the parking lot. All of us were heading to Jack's Pizza, but when the other kid saw there weren't any adults around, he started jabbing at Travis again. Travis must have been twice his size, but the kid started pounding away."

Chip was breathing hard, and I could tell he was fighting back tears.

"I ran over to them and got in between and shoved them apart. I told them to stop. The kid from Bakersfield calmed down, but Travis yelled at me to mind my own business. He cursed at me the whole time, walking backward down the curb and across the street. We shouted for him to stop, but it was too late. There was a car coming. The driver hardly had a chance to put his brakes on."

Chip stopped. He was resting his elbows on his legs, his face looking down. I saw a tear hit the linoleum floor. "If only I hadn't tried to stop them, Travis wouldn't have got all riled up, and he'd have stayed on the sidewalk." Chip covered his face with his hands.

I reached out and held his shoulder. "It's all

right, Chip. Hey, it's not your fault. You did the right thing."

He picked up his head and looked at me. "I know you're right," he said. "Anybody else would have done the same. I told myself that all night, but I guess I had to hear it from someone else. Thanks, Darcy."

"What are friends for? Besides, I know exactly how you feel."

I told Chip about my failure to deliver the supplies on time and about the scene in ER. I was surprised when tears started to fill my eyes too, as I explained that I still felt as though it would be my fault if Travis didn't pull through. We let our eyes hold each other as we both realized we were drawn together in this whole crazy thing.

"Do you think he'll make it?" Chip asked.

It was about time for someone to sweep the sadness out of the air. "I think so. And hey, he's got me!" I said, putting a cheery slant on my words.

"Huh?" Chip gave me a puzzled look.

"I work there, remember? I promise I'll be a good candy striper and see that he pulls through. I'll take good care of him for you. For us both."

Chip smiled.

The entire school was buzzing Monday morning with talk about Travis. There was no news about his condition, so the rumors got wild. Some had him coming back to school the next day. Others said he'd be in a coma the rest of his life. The rumors changed with each new class period.

There were also stories about how the accident happened. One had Travis getting into a fight with a high schooler who hit him with a bat. Another had him being struck by a bus after a kid pushed him into the street. Unfortunately for Chip, the worst of the stories picked on him. He was accused of tripping Travis into the oncoming traffic in one story and blamed for not rescuing him in the next.

When lunch time finally rolled around and Chip sat down with Mandy, April, and me, he was really upset.

"I know what you said, Darcy, but I still believe that if I had only kept my nose out of it, Travis wouldn't have backed out into the street the way he did."

"Look at it this way," Mandy tried to encourage him. "If you hadn't broken up the fight, Travis might have beat up the other kid really bad. Or maybe the guy would have knocked out Travis's lights."

"Yeah, maybe," Chip groaned as he pushed aside his sandwich, "but there's no way either of them would have hit hard enough to put anybody in a coma."

"Oh, get a life!" April burst out. She had been quietly peeling a banana, just listening, which was unusual for April. But apparently she had heard enough. "The problem with you, Chip, is that you're always doing the right thing. You hardly ever do anything wrong, and everybody knows it. When something goes haywire and you're involved, you can't handle it!"

Our table was dead quiet.

April crumpled up her trash, stood up, and announced, "Sorry, but I'm outta here. I see Julie Baxter on the other side. I've got to check out what she's wearing. It's the ugliest thing you'd ever want to see." She picked up her tray and walked away.

I looked at Mandy. We both realized that April had just uttered one of the more mature things she'd ever said in her life—her comment about Chip, that is, not her remark about Julie Baxter's outfit.

Chip stared at the empty space she had occupied.

"She's right, you know," I softly said. "You did the right thing. You can never blame yourself when you do the right thing."

Chip finally smiled a true Chip smile, the first I'd seen in several days.

"Wanna finish my Twinkie?" he asked me.

Mom drove me to the hospital after school. I sat in the back next to my folded wheelchair while Josh hugged the front window, preoccupied with a Batman comic book. It was a short but quiet drive.

I would have bundled up and wheeled myself had it not been for the icy wind. It swept away the thin layer of snow on the ground, making it look as though it was flurrying again. It was not a day to be outside, especially in a wheelchair.

But it was more than the weather that forced me to ride with my mom. I felt all funny inside—an uneasy, restless feeling—and I just wanted to be with her. As we got closer to the hospital, I felt sick to my stomach. I leaned up over the front seat to be closer to Mom and Josh, and I broke out in a cold sweat. Mom turned down the heat, but that only made me shiver. One of my legs got the shakes and I couldn't control it. My foot bounced up and down.

Why am I feeling this way? Am I getting sick? Am I upset about Chip? about Travis? Maybe I'm afraid of going back to the hospital and getting in trouble for what I did. I'm so confused.

Then just before we rounded the corner to the hospital, Mom did a very "parent" thing. She pulled the car off the side of the road and turned off the engine.

Josh put down his comic book and gave her an exasperated look. "Mo-o-m, why are we stopping?"

My mother just sat there, holding onto the steering wheel and staring straight ahead while Josh kicked underneath the front dash with his foot. She turned and gave him a serious look and, without anymore complaints, he went back to his comic book.

Then she looked in the rearview mirror. I was surprised to see that her eyes looked ready to spill tears. She spoke softly to me, sounding afraid.

"Darcy, I'm not feeling well, and you don't look well either," she said.

The mirror was small, and all I saw were her eyes. They were now crying.

"How did you know?" I asked.

"Because I'm remembering what things were

like when you had your accident. You are too, aren't you?" The car was quiet for a moment. The only sound was Josh swinging his feet and a gust or two of wind outside.

Mom took a deep breath, wiped her eyes, and went on, "This ride to the hospital to see Travis, and the plans that you're making to help him—that's how I remember Monica talking about you. And the way everyone prayed at church yesterday for the McAllister family. It's so strange . . . it's all coming back."

Cars streamed by us, spraying slush on the side of our car.

Josh sat quietly, flipping the pages of his comic book. He looked at Mom, then at me. "Is everything okay?" he asked.

"Yes, everything's okay. It's just that—" Mom got choked up. She reached over and stroked Josh's hair.

I spoke up. "It'll be okay. Really. This accident isn't happening to me or any one of us. It's happening to Travis and his family. And we can do something about it. We can help, right?"

Mom looked at me in the mirror again. Her eyes were still red, but I sensed a smile. The funny feeling in my stomach was disappearing.

"Yes, Darcy, you're right. This isn't about us. Thanks for reminding me. Let's go." She started up the engine and turned the corner into the hospital drive.

Within minutes, Mom had unfolded my wheelchair, hoisted me into it, and waved me off. I sped through the automatic glass doors and headed to Miss Graf's desk.

I donned my candy striper jacket, rolled up my sleeves, and plunged into my job with new excitement. Cruising down the hospital hallway, at last I felt like I had a task that I knew I could do. I could help Travis get better. I could tend to his needs and maybe even do some therapy stuff with him.

I knew I still had my other jobs to do, but even stuffing envelopes and dusting filing cabinets didn't seem so bad. Not delivering the syringes when I should have on Saturday had showed me just how important my job was to everyone—especially the patients. I moved more quickly, smiled a lot, and offered to help with a variety of odds and ends that I used to moan about.

My new attitude did not go unnoticed.

"Feeling good today, Darcy?" the janitor asked as I passed him in the hallway mopping the floor.

"Sure thing. Don't you just love working here?" I asked, a little surprised at my own question.

"You got that right," he said. "Have a good day now."

Miss Graf caught up with me after I delivered the mail. "Darcy, would you mind going down to the cafeteria? I know it's a distasteful job, but they need someone to clean the trays off before they go through the washing machine."

"No problem," I answered.

"You sure?"

"Yeah, I'm sure. I'll go right now. And Miss Graf?"

"Yes?"

"I'm sorry for having a bad attitude about my work. I'll do better from now on."

Miss Graf folded her arms and gave me a smile. "That's nice of you to say, Darcy. I was beginning to wonder whether or not you were cut out for being a candy striper. Keep it up."

I smiled back, proud of myself for making a change and proud that someone had noticed it.

I wasted no time taking the elevator down to the cafeteria. The job was ickier than I imagined, and it took every ounce of joy in me to get through it. I couldn't believe what adults did with leftover food! Chocolate pudding mixed with French dressing, cottage cheese dumped on a pile of spaghetti sauce, peanut butter and peas dumped together. Yuck.

As messy as it was, it didn't take long to scrape off all the trays. "Am I done now?" I asked the kitchen supervisor. I hoped she would say yes, but I was willing to stay if needed.

"Yep, looks that way. Thanks for the help!"

"Yesss!" I cheered as I threw my apron into the laundry basket. I had the rest of the afternoon all planned out. It was time, I figured, to take on some real nursing responsibilities. I buzzed Miss Graf on the phone.

"May I visit Travis McAllister at ICU now? My job down here is done."

"I'd be happy to let you go up there, but I'm sure they won't let you in, Darcy. You need to be a relative to see someone in the intensive care unit." She could sense my disappointment on the phone and added, "You can stop by the desk and see how he's doing, though."

I hung up the phone and made my way to the second floor. The intensive care unit, or ICU, is where they keep everyone who has something seriously wrong with them, like right after surgeries or car accidents. I turned the corner into the unit. I could hear breathing machines whooshing and monitors beeping in the rooms down the hallway. There were nurses everywhere. Only the nurses' station separated me from all the action.

"Hi. I'm Darcy DeAngelis. I was wondering how Travis was and if I could see him."

"Are you his sister?" the nurse at the desk asked.

"No. I'm a candy striper here." I pointed to my uniform.

"Yes, I see that." The nurse thought for a moment. "We don't normally let people other than family in, but since you're one of the staff, I suppose I could let you in for a minute. But just this once. The regular head nurse comes back tomorrow. She might be a little more strict."

The nurse got up and led me to the room where they had put Travis. "He's doing better. His parents are here, too."

She stopped at the doorway of a small room and motioned me in. I wheeled a couple of feet in and halted by the bathroom door. Travis was directly in front of me, lying on a tall bed. His right leg was outside the sheets, propped up on pillows and encased in a white plaster cast. There were tubes connected to all parts of his body and a special one connected to his right arm. A bandage covered his head and his left eye. The other eye was closed. Everything about him looked painful. His chest and arms had bruises and scrapes.

I shuddered at the sight, remembering the tall, handsome Travis I had met in the hallway at school the week before. Except for the sandy hair that stuck out from under the bandage, I would have thought the nurse had made a mistake as to who this was.

Mr. and Mrs. McAllister were seated in lounge chairs. Both of them were sleeping, obviously tired from waiting up nights with their son to see whether or not he would regain consciousness. I didn't want to disturb anyone, so I sat for a long moment listening to the beeping of the machine next to his bed.

I fixed my eyes on Travis and bowed my head.

Lord, I don't know why Travis is here, but I pray that he'll get better soon. Watch over his parents and encourage them, too. Help me to be a friend to Travis the way you want me to. In Jesus' name. Amen.

I said my prayer inside my head so as not to wake the McAllisters or Travis, but it was as if Mrs. McAllister had read my mind while she slept. She opened her eyes and smiled at me.

She whispered, "Hello. What's your name?"

I leaned forward and whispered back, "Darcy. Darcy De Angelis. I work here. I mean I'm a volunteer. I go to the same school as Travis. We met last week. How is he?"

"Well." Mrs. McAllister sighed and shifted in her

chair. "We're not sure. He regained consciousness yesterday morning."

"Like around church time?" I asked eagerly. "Our pastor prayed for Travis then."

"Well, wasn't that sweet of you and your friends?" Mrs. McAllister was polite but looked as though she didn't really understand. "Anyway, he fell back asleep a little while later. He's been asleep ever since."

"He'll be all right," I said. "I did that too when I had my accident. It was really weird. Kind of like being in a long dream and wanting to wake up, but you can't. The doctor said it was a way for my body to get a chance to heal without having the pain."

"Is that so?" Travis' mother seemed interested in my story. As I continued explaining, it seemed like I was really helping, the way a clinical psychologist would. She looked at me several times, top to bottom while I spoke.

"I see," she said, nodding. "What's your name again?"

"Darcy. I'm in seventh grade. Travis is a really good basketball player."

"Yes, well, thank you."

We both realized basketball didn't mean much at that point, and our eyes looked away from each other and toward Travis.

"I guess I'd better go." I could tell my welcome had lasted long enough. Mrs. McAllister seemed more interested in watching her son than in listening to a twelve-year-old talk.

"Say hi to Travis for me when he wakes up."

She nodded her head absentmindedly and rose up to sit on the bed beside Travis. She held his hand and looked at his face. There was an obvious look of worry mixed with love around her eyes.

I left the room and went back to the first floor where I picked up my coat. My first day as a *real* candy striper was over.

6

That week, after I finished all my filing jobs each day, I headed for ICU. The regular head nurse followed the rules to the letter. Even though she knew how badly I wanted to see Travis, I was only allowed to go to the visiting room and talk with his mom. Mrs. McAllister seemed to enjoy reporting his progress to me, and it made me feel like I was fulfilling a useful role. Besides that, we were getting to know each other.

On Thursday, she tracked me down in the hallway of the fourth floor. "He's awake!" she said excitedly. "Travis is awake! The doctor says he's going to make it."

"I knew it!" I let out a whoop and looked up to the ceiling. "Thanks, Lord."

I breezed through the rest of my duties, whistling as I worked. On Friday I took the elevator to the second floor to visit ICU again, but when I looked past the nurses' station, I saw that they were moving Travis's bed and things out of his room. My heart leapt in fear.

"Where's Travis?" I asked the ICU secretary.

"Travis? Oh, he's been moved."

I breathed a sigh of relief. For a second I had thought he'd died. "Where to?" I asked.

"Fourth floor, I think. Not sure which room. Check with the nurses there."

"Fourth floor? That's my floor! Yesss!" I cheered to myself as I wheeled back to the elevator. Now I could really help.

I hurried back and sped to the nurses' station to check on his room number. Mrs. McAllister happened to be there, talking with Miss Graf.

"Hi, Mrs. McAllister," I said.

"Well, hello, Darcy!" Her smile was wide. She looked rested and much more beautiful than I remembered. I could see where Travis got his good looks.

"Come with me," she said. "I'll take you to Travis's room. I'm sure he'll be happy to see you. He's talking now and moving his arms. It won't be long till he's sitting up." She explained his condition to me on the way down.

"The doctor said Travis will walk eventually, once the swelling of his brain goes down. He'll have to work hard though, and go through therapy." She hesitated and looked down at my wheelchair. "But I guess you know all about that. When will you be done with your therapy and walk again, Darcy?"

I didn't get upset with her question. She just didn't know. "Well, you see, my accident was a little

70

different. It smashed my spinal cord, which means my legs can't get signals from my brain. My paralysis is permanent. I'll never walk again."

"Oh. I'm sorry. I . . ." She was embarrassed.

I tried hard to think of a way to make her feel better. "But maybe they'll discover a way to fix it through research and then, you know, I could walk someday."

"Oh, I hope so, dear," she said sincerely.

"In the meantime, just be happy for Travis."

Mrs. McAllister nodded gratefully as we stopped by the door of Room 415. "Well, here it is!" She entered ahead of me and cheerfully announced our presence to her son. "Here's one of your girlfriends from school, sweetheart. She's been visiting you every single day."

Travis looked more like himself without all those bandages and tubes. His eyes, eager to see this visitor his mother had been talking about, squinted as I entered the room.

"Who are you?" he asked, almost with a sneer.

I was embarrassed, not only by his question, but also by his mother's announcement that I was one of his girlfriends.

"I'm Darcy. We met a couple of weeks ago. In the lobby before classes started. You know . . . I'm the one with the dog?"

"Oh, yeah, the dog!" Travis' face lit up a little friendlier. "I remember. He was a cool dog. Is he here?"

"At the hospital?"

"Yeah, why not?" he asked, sounding as though

he owned the place.

"Well, you just can't bring a dog in here. It isn't allowed."

He changed the subject. "You work here?"

"Well, kind of. I'm a candy striper."

He didn't say anything, but I thought I heard a snicker. It was obvious he didn't think much of candy stripers. What an attitude!

Travis looked away toward the window. The sun was washing through the open shades.

"Close the stupid shades, will ya, Mom?" he ordered.

Mrs. McAllister jumped up and pulled the shades shut. "Is that better, dear?" she asked.

"Yeah." There was a few seconds of silence, and then he piped up, "When is dinner gonna be here? I'm hungry."

"In a little while, sweetheart," she answered, sitting back down.

"What are they going to give me?"

"Just liquids, I think. Jell-O and soup."

Travis wrinkled his face and complained about the food, then about the heat, and then about the sheets. It was as though he wanted to make sure everybody knew that he was back in control. Or at least, he hoped so. It was also obvious he was ignoring me.

"I should go," I finally said. "It's getting near five when my mom picks me up. May I visit tomorrow?"

"Whatever," Travis answered. He closed his eyes and laid his head back on the pillow, his face showing pain.

I looked to Mrs. McAllister to see if she thought I should come back, but she only looked at her son. I wheeled back out of the room without saying good-bye. Saying anything at that point would have been the wrong thing to do.

Once in the hallway, I wheeled across the hall to Mrs. Hamlin's. She was sitting in her chair again, this time knitting.

"I just wanted to tell you something," I said. "Remember the boy I told you about? Travis? He's been moved to a room across the hall from you. Isn't that great?"

"Oh, yes, dear. That's wonderful. Giving him plenty of Vitamin 13, I hope."

"Huh?"

"You know, I Corinthians 13." She put down the needles and yarn on her lap. "It's been working for you, hasn't it? The nurses say you're a new girl. A happier girl."

"I guess so," I said. "Although it didn't help much today. Travis seemed angry when he saw me. He cares more about EJ, my dog, than about me."

"Now remember—" her voice rose as she raised that crooked finger.

"I know," I stopped her. "Love doesn't keep track of wrongs."

"That's right. And don't forget, now that you're truly loving someone, try to find creative ways to show it. Love isn't so much an emotion as it is an action. Remember that." She looked at her watch. "Oops. You better run along before you're late meeting your mother. It's about that time, isn't it?"

I looked at my watch too. It was five minutes to five. "Yikes!" I exclaimed. "See you tomorrow." I headed out the door, and Mrs. Hamlin returned to her knitting.

As I cruised toward the elevator, I thought about Mrs. Hamlin's instructions to find a creative way to love. Suddenly a brilliant idea burst into my brain. *Darcy DeAngelis, you are a genius!*

I stopped at the nurses' station and parked myself beside it. In my most mature and responsible tone of voice I said, "Miss Graf?"

She turned toward me with a questioning look.

With a sly and confident smile I asked, "Do you think I could bring my service dog, EJ, tomorrow? I take him into all kinds of places. I was just thinking about how Travis loves that dog. Seeing EJ would really help Travis, I think."

Miss Graf's mouth hung open. "You want to bring your dog to the hospital?!"

"EJ's really clean, Miss Graf, and he won't get in the way. I promise. Just for thirty minutes. Please?"

She shook her head. "Dogs don't belong in a hospital. Where did you even get such an idea?"

I wasn't about to give in. This was too good an idea to drop. "Service dogs do this kind of thing all the time. They're trained to be in places like this. And besides, I'm trying to think of a way to cheer up Travis. He really seems to like EJ."

Dr. Vanderhook was standing nearby. I knew he could hear our conversation.

"Actually, it might not be a bad idea," he interrupted, flopping his chart on Miss Graf's desk.

74

"Travis has a pretty bad attitude right now. I know it's not hospital policy, but what if Darcy tried it? She could bring the dog down to the solarium on the first floor through the outside entrance. It would do the young man some good. I know Darcy here, and I've watched EJ operate around town. He's quite a dog."

Miss Graf didn't have a prayer against Dr. Vanderhook. He was one of those grandfather types who made you feel better without medicine. Just his easy manner did the trick.

"If you say so, Doctor," Miss Graf replied. She turned to me, saying, "I'll let the McAllisters know. Bring the dog at eleven o'clock tomorrow morning. I'll have Travis at the solarium." She couldn't believe what she was saying. She rolled her eyes and went back to the papers on her desk, saying, "Who knows, maybe we'll start a zoo here next week."

"Thanks," I said as I bolted toward the elevator. "See you tomorrow."

The next day I spent the entire morning getting EJ ready for his visit with Travis. I combed out his hair, squirted extra drops of dog mouthwash in his food, put on his newer collar, and fitted him with his cleanest service dog harness.

Getting EJ ready was a lot simpler than getting myself ready. I felt fat. My jeans looked all frumpy. My hair didn't go the way I wanted it to. And the bright Saturday morning sun made my skin look pale and showed up all my freckles and zits. On top of that, I got angry at my feet again. They were badly swollen and looked more paralyzed than usual.

What made me boil hotter was that I knew why I was angry. On any other Saturday morning I would have felt easy and breezy. I would have cared less how I looked. But this was no ordinary Saturday. I was going to see Travis today—tall, handsome, popular eighth grader—and that meant I had to look like anything other than a short, ugly, shy seventh grader. I was mad at myself for being so self-conscious. So self-aware. Self-absorbed. So full of . . . self!

By ten-thirty I had pulled my entire wardrobe out of my closet, trying on this and that and then throwing everything on the bed in disgust. I had combed my hair every which way and used enough zit cream to cover acres of acne.

EJ seemed bored by it all. He waited quietly on the floor with his head resting on his paw.

Our station wagon pulled up beside the entrance of the hospital at eleven o'clock sharp.

"See ya later, Mom," I said as I quickly slid into my chair, slammed the car door, and let EJ begin pulling me to the door.

"Don't you want me to come in?" she asked. "What if you need help with that heavy door?"

"Mom!" I complained. I had no way of explaining how I felt about her joining me. I couldn't tell her I wanted to be alone with Travis and that having Mommy around would make me look like a third grader. All I could do was give a dumb excuse. "I don't think it's a good idea for too many people to be in there. EJ might get nervous or something. Or Travis might not be ready for so many people."

I was fishing and Mom knew it, but she understood. She just said, "I'll meet you back here at noon. Enough time?"

"Yeah, sure thing." I waved and rolled into the hospital, eager to get out of the cold wind and into the warm solarium.

The solarium was a room with glass on all sides and skylights all over the ceiling. Green plants cascaded over the window sills. A bird cage hung from the ceiling, and two singing canaries made it feel out-of-doors. It was a warm and relaxing place to spend a morning, and I could see why patients often used the solarium to get away from their boring rooms.

What a shock I got when I entered the room. A boom box blared in the corner. There were kids everywhere, some sitting on the windowsill eating pizza, and others in a huddle on the floor playing cards. I recognized some kids from Jordan Junior High, including a few basketball players and a couple of cheerleaders. They were all laughing and having a good time. The smell of chili fries and onion rings filled the air.

Travis was dressed in a blue bathrobe and seated in a large hospital wheelchair. A single bandage circled his head. His face wasn't pale anymore, and he was laughing and scarfing down pizza with everyone else. He hardly looked as though he'd been in an accident.

I felt out of place as I looked around the room. It was obvious Travis's friends had planned a party,

77

and I wondered why Miss Graf hadn't told me. I almost headed back outside to see if I could catch Mom, but a voice stopped me.

"Hey, EJ!" Travis yelled out.

EJ obeyed the call and pulled me back in Travis's direction. I held on to the leather strap as he dragged me through the crowd of eighth graders. Everybody parted as if we were Moses and Aaron walking through the Red Sea.

"Lay off the music, will ya!" Travis called out. Someone flicked the knob, and the silence made our approach all the more dramatic. My heart beat furiously. All eyes were on EJ and me.

"The nurse said you'd bring him. Thanks," Travis said as he leaned forward in his wheelchair, extending his hand. "Come here, EJ."

I let go of my dog. EJ and Travis greeted one another like old friends. For the next hour I was pretty much out of the picture except for giving EJ his commands to do tricks and stuff. I led him through a series of jobs. He fetched things, turned the lights on and off, sat on Travis's lap, and even played dead. Then after Travis had had his turn, I did the same routine for other kids. It felt like show -and-tell.

During the entire hour no one talked to me or noticed my presence, except as I related to EJ. It was as if I were not there at all. And when it came time to leave, no one said good-bye—that is, except to EJ.

As I headed out, Travis was swallowed up again in the crowd of basketball buddies and cheerleaders.

Nothing of him was showing except his feet resting on the footrests of the wheelchair. It was a reminder to me that the only thing I'd ever have in common with Travis McAllister was our wheelchairs, at least for the time being.

Wake up, Darcy! You're not in the same world as he is.

That's why when the phone rang that night, and Monica yelled, "Darcy, it's Travis!" I was stunned.

I grabbed the phone, took a deep breath, and put on my best "Oh, it's you" tone of voice.

"Hi, this is Travis. Are you busy?" His voice sounded tired to me.

"Uh, no. I was just watching TV. What's up? Are you okay?"

"Kinda. I'm a little tired. The party wore me out. And I got sick to my stomach from the pizza and fries."

"Umm. Too much spicy stuff."

"Yeah. Too much spice."

I couldn't believe I was on the phone with Travis talking about oregano and chili peppers. But I didn't know why else he called, so I just charged ahead.

"I wondered about that food. I'm surprised Miss Graf didn't smell all the garlic and come down to the solarium and chase everybody out. You probably weren't supposed to be eating that kind of stuff."

"I know."

"Seemed like you had a good time, though."

"I guess. Listen, I wanted to thank you for bringing EJ today. He was a lot of fun. It made me feel better."

"I'm glad he could help. He makes me feel better, too." There was silence at both ends of the phone. And with the silence, I realized that Travis considered me more than just an acquaintance.

"The doctor says I can start therapy," Travis said, changing the subject. "He thinks I should start walking soon. That's why I called. Do you think you could help me? You've been through therapy before, right?"

"Uh-huh. I'd love to help. I know all about the equipment there. When do you start?"

"Not till the end of next week, I think. He wants the stitches in my head to come out first."

"Yeah, you wouldn't want to burst your stitches when you flex your muscles!" I kidded. I sounded like April when she's at her bubble-headed best, or worst, as the case may be. I cringed.

Travis mumbled something I didn't catch and then said. "Well, I better hang up. The nurse has to give me something. See ya next week, okay?"

"Okay. See ya."

I gently hung up the phone and looked at EJ, who was sitting next to me wagging his tail.

"Guess what, EJ? Travis didn't once ask how you were doing!"

Travis had called *me*, not my dog!

7

It was a Saturday night every girl should enjoy once in a while. I was all cozy in my room and pillow-propped comfortably against the headboard. My favorite Amy Grant album played softly in the background and a mug of hot chocolate sat next to me on my side table. My good old Box rested on my lap, its contents spilling all over the quilt.

My Box was my own kind of diary stuffed with favorite memories including old movie tickets, photos of EJ as a pup, special class notes, a fistful of my letters wrapped in a rubber band, and a snippet of horse hair from one of my favorite ponies at Willowbrook Stables.

The newest addition to the Box was a journal Mom had given me. In it I could write anything I wanted, including letters to God. The journal was like a friend.

It's the little things, I jotted on a clean page before nestling down to sleep.

It's the little things like phone calls that can change how you see things. I spent all afternoon feeling depressed about the visit with Travis at the hospital. And then in just one hour, I'm happier than a kid at Christmas. Why can't all my days be full of little things like phone calls? Why can't God arrange it that way all the time?

I knew the adults in my life would have an answer to my question. They'd say something like, "You can't have happy things happen all the time," or "Bad days help you grow in character." Probably God would say the same thing. I was a little afraid of hearing His answer.

I kept writing.

I'm tired of bad things always happening. And I'm tired of grown up lectures about turning tough times into triumph. That's the kind of boring stuff you hear in church.

A pang of guilt struck me squarely and I quickly scribbled more.

I didn't mean that, Lord. It's just that sometimes I'd rather not listen in church. Will You forgive me? I know You understand. I really like my church.

I had to be careful not to get all self-centered in my letters. With the phone call from Travis fresh on my mind, it was too tempting to let my thoughts run away with the pen in my hand. I put my pen and journal back into my Box and took one last sip of hot chocolate. I was glad God was the only one who would see my journal. But sometimes I embarrassed myself in front of Him with the dumb things I wrote. I was also glad God gave forgiveness as well as a balanced perspective on things like surprise phone calls from cute older boys. I flicked off my bedside lamp and settled down underneath the covers, thanking God for bringing me back to reality.

I went to church the next morning looking forward to telling my friends what had happened. I especially wanted to see Chip. I made a point of sitting next to him before the worship service started, parking my wheelchair at the end of his aisle. We whispered as loudly as we could above the sound of the organ.

"So how is Travis?" he asked.

"Really great. They had a party at the hospital yesterday. And he called me last night!"

"He called you?" Chip seemed surprised.

"Yeah," I said, as if it were no big deal. "He wants me to help him with his therapy later this week. He'll be out of the hospital soon, I bet."

"Did he say anything about me?" Chip asked.

"No, not really. He hasn't talked about the accident at all."

"Well, when do you think I could see him? I want to apologize for butting into the fight."

I stopped for a moment. I felt bad for Chip and wanted him to be able to get this thing behind him. But I didn't want anything, or anyone, to get Travis upset. Especially now. I was just getting to know Travis. Chip might spoil that.

"Tell you what," I said. "I'll see how he's doing during the week and soften him up a bit before you see him. That way it'll be easier for you. What do you think?"

Chip nodded and smiled. Then he did one of those unexpected little things. He reached over to my lap and squeezed my hand softly. "Thanks for being a good friend," he whispered close to my ear.

My mind raced with all kinds of thoughts, and my heart wrestled with all sorts of feelings. I felt guilty for not telling Chip the real reason I didn't want him to see Travis right away. I had made it sound like I was doing Chip a favor, but in fact, I really wanted extra time with Travis. Besides guilt, I also felt embarrassed—did anyone see Chip squeeze my hand? Then again, I felt special that Chip would show me affection that way.

A tap on my shoulder from behind made me jump in my seat. It was Mandy. She passed me a note while we sang the first song.

Hey, cut it out, you two. Valentine's Day isn't here yet!

My face turned red and I quickly crumpled up the note, hoping Chip hadn't seen it. I turned around and looked up at Mandy who was holding her hymn book in front of her face. She moved it to reveal a knowing smile.

After the service, when the pastor was praying and everybody was standing with their heads bowed and eyes closed, I made my escape. My heart and mind had been battling for the full hour, and I had hardly listened to the sermon. At that point I didn't want to face Chip or Mandy. I just wanted to be alone.

Monday afternoon found me in my candy striper uniform heading for the fourth floor. I was surprised to learn that the doctor had changed his mind about when Travis could start physical therapy. Travis had already begun. I immediately headed to the PT room and found him working with weights from his wheelchair. I wheeled up and parked my chair across from his, giving him the thumbs-up as he strained and sweat. His body was weak, and he looked as though he might faint.

I didn't want to sound like a nag, so I just said "Keep it up, guy" and rolled up my sleeves and flexed my own biceps. Travis grinned and strained with his weights all the harder. I knew he'd fall for the challenge, being such a competitor!

Day after day we sat together in physical therapy. I watched and encouraged him most of the time; once in a while I grabbed a couple of weights and exercised alongside him. It took us a few days to warm up to each other and be really comfortable talking, but by Thursday I could tell that Travis looked forward to our time together each day.

"So how's school?" he asked as we wheeled into the PT room Thursday afternoon.

"Okay, I guess. My classes seem easy right now, even though it's still boring. Did you hear about the false alarm? It was great. We had to stay out in the courtyard for an hour while the fire trucks came. It was wild!"

We parked next to the weight machine.

"Wish I'd been there," Travis said.

"Everyone at school talks about you," I said, changing the subject. "They're glad to hear you're progressing."

He moved from his chair onto the narrow bench and grabbed hold of the handle of the barbells.

"Me, too," he said. "Except it hurts. It gives me a headache."

"Yeah, but you're getting stronger every day. I have to add more and more weights to the machine all the time. Look here, you started at twenty pounds and you're up to forty already."

"Forty. Big deal. I used to be able to do 120. Forty is for wimps." He pushed up on the handle and by sheer anger made the machine hit against the top and then slam down as he released it. He wiped his mouth and glared at his wheelchair beside him. "I'll never get out of that thing," he said, pointing to it. He pushed up again on the weights.

"Of course you'll walk again. There's nothing wrong with you except a broken leg and your head injuries. Both will heal, I'm sure."

Travis leaned over to rub his knees. He grimaced as he touched a sore spot. "I'm not so sure. My legs just feel weird—like they don't have any strength at all. Even the one that's not broken. And look at you . . . after all, you didn't ever walk again."

I didn't answer. He knew the difference in our injuries, but he was too angry at that point to admit it.

"Trust me," I said softly. "You'll walk again. We just need to get you up on those crutches."

"Crutches! Humph! As for walking, I hope you're right. And if I don't, at least I'll have one friend."

I turned my head to one side, not understanding what he meant.

"You don't care about my wheelchair," he explained. "You understand. But if I don't walk or play basketball again, who else will want to hang out with me?"

I was a little hurt by what Travis said, but I understood. I had felt that way before. "Maybe. Maybe not. We'll have to see."

Friday brought Travis closer to the day when he'd walk again . . . and closer to me. Still, though, I had a hard time getting him to try his crutches. At the close of Friday's PT session, we were both exhausted. But not too exhausted to have some fun.

"Wanna race?" he asked as we wheeled out of the therapy room. "The solarium is the finish line!"

"You're on. But I warn you, my chair's a lot better than that hospital one you're using."

"Who cares? On your mark, get set, go!" Travis said quickly. It gave him a chance to pull away before I was ready. By the time I finally did get moving, he was ten feet ahead.

Fortunately for me, my sport chair was better for racing—it was a customized job with super ball bearings, a well-oiled frame, and racing tires angled in so I could get a good grip on the cork-wrapped rims. Besides that, five years of pushing the chair had made my skinny arms pretty muscular.

I caught up to Travis as we sped past rooms, water fountains, and offices. We almost crashed into an orderly.

"Watch where you're going!" we heard his voice yell after us.

By the time I reached the solarium I was a good fifteen feet ahead of Travis. I grabbed the handle of the open solarium door and used it to help make a quick spin into the room. When Travis glided in a few seconds later, I faced him triumphantly, arms folded across my chest.

We both laughed while we tried to catch our breath. I looked at the empty room around us. The sun was setting in a bright orange glow that cast a golden color over everything in the room. With green plants everywhere, it looked like our own little forest.

"You're really fast," he finally said, still breathing heavily.

"Like I said, my chair is a lot better than yours. Hospitals don't give you a model like mine just to get you from room to room." I didn't want Travis to think I was too good. After all, I was there to encourage him, not to show him up and make him feel like a wimp.

Travis, however, was not finished being impressed with me.

"What else can you do in your chair besides race?" he asked.

"Let's see." I thought for a moment and made

my way to the center of the room. I pulled back on the wheels and tilted my chair up, allowing the front wheels to swing in the air. Like the Lone Ranger on Silver, I precariously balanced to hold my chair in a "rearing up" position.

"How do you do that?"

"I just pull back and then keep my weight over the back wheels."

"I'm going to try it," he said.

"Be careful; your cast might keep you off balance."

"Hey, no sweat. I do this on my bike all the time."

I watched as Travis made a couple of unsuccessful attempts. On the third try he managed to hold it for a few seconds.

"Ta da!" he announced proudly.

I laughed and clapped. "You're really good!"

He was pleased with himself. "What else can you teach me?"

My heart pounded with joy. Travis not only didn't mind my wheelchair, but he made it a lot of fun. Suddenly I could be someone totally unique, someone no one else could be. And it was someone a guy like Travis thought was outta sight!

I balanced on the two rear wheels again and, by moving my hands in opposite directions, made the chair spin around in a full circle. It was like pulling back on a horse and making him spin around on his two hind legs. My chair came to a crashing rest after I finished the circle.

Travis didn't wait for any instruction. As soon as

my wheels met the floor, he tried it. Unfortunately his first jerk of the wheels was too hard. He and his chair flew backward and hit against the couch behind him. Travis lay limp in a twisted, awkward position, half in his chair and half on the couch.

"Oh, no!" I panicked. I figured he must have hit his head and was unconscious. I swung around to get help.

"No!" Travis cried out. "I'm okay, really. I just hit my shoulder." He was in pain, but his voice reassured me. I wheeled closer to him.

His wheelchair was still back on two legs and looked like it would slip off the couch and crash to the floor any minute. "Darcy . . . come . . . come over here so I can hold on to your wheelchair."

I got as close to him as I could and locked my brakes securely. Nervously, I held out my arms. He grabbed my hands and pulled. His body sank down into the chair, causing the front of it to slam on to the floor.

"Aaugh!" His eyes shut tight against the pain, and he slumped his head onto my shoulder, breathless and shaking.

I put my arm around him and held him as tightly as I dared.

For a long moment we rested that way while Travis' breathing and shaking calmed down. The solarium was quiet except for the light fluttering of the canary's wings. I looked outside just in time to see the sun set below the horizon of snow, its rays painting glorious colors in the winter sky.

Travis gave a big sigh. The pain was passing. He

sat up straight, and I loosened my hold around his shoulder. We looked at each other. His eyes were still moist with tears from the pain.

I don't know how long we looked at each other, but I began to feel uncomfortable. While a part of me liked the feeling, another part of me didn't.

"Does this mean you'll use crutches from now on?" I kidded.

He smiled. Then he leaned over from his chair and kissed me on the cheek.

At least I think it was a kiss, I wrote in my journal that night. *It was kind of hard to tell because he did it so fast and my hair got in the way a little. Just more like a touch with his lips, I think. Why did he do that?*

For the second time in a row, I concluded my journal entry with a question.

It had been one of those little things again. Little things that made me feel good . . . and a little scared. What next?

8

In the cafeteria on Monday, I sat moping while my friends ate their lunch. I gave away half my hot dog and all my fruit cup. I moved the last remaining french fry on my plate in a figure eight through the catsup.

"So, what's the matter with you today?" April asked at last.

"Nothing."

"Yeah, right," she said. "You're sitting there with a 'poor me' look all over your face, and you say there's nothing the matter. Get real. Hey, Mandy, let's cheer this kid up. I'm getting deee-pressed real fast by our friend here."

My attempt at giving April a dirty look was hardly worthwhile.

"Yeah, Darcy," Mandy said. "You do seem out of it. What's up?"

"Nothing. I just don't feel good."

"Are you sick?" another girl asked.

"Don't answer that," April interrupted. "I figured it out!" She held out her arms, and everyone got quiet. Then, as if making an announcement to the world, she proclaimed, "Darcy is in love!"

All the girls at the table burst out laughing. I mustered a laugh too, hoping to hide my feelings. It wasn't that I was in love. And it wasn't that I wasn't in love. I just didn't know what was happening. The only thing I knew was that I had to hide my mixed-up feelings. I couldn't bear having April or anyone else spread rumors or make fun of me.

"Yeah, right!" I added when the laugher died down. "And I'm going to walk tomorrow!"

The girls seemed to accept my denial, but April wasn't fooled. She pried further.

"Been spending a lot of time with Travis, haven't you?" she asked on the sly. "What goes on between you two? And just what does PT stand for, anyway . . . Passionate and Tender?"

"Get outta here," I joked. But inside I was panicking. *Lord, get me out of this mess!* Fortunately, the very idea of Travis and me going out together was too unbelievable for anyone sitting around the table.

"Travis and Darcy?" one girl guffawed loudly. "Better chance of there being no school the rest of the year!"

Everyone laughed again and added their own comments and jokes. April's idea was rejected, and I felt safe.

"C'mon, girls," April finally said, picking up her tray to leave. "Let's go check out the courtyard."

The others got up to follow her, leaving Mandy and me alone at the lunch table.

"So what's really the matter, Darcy?" Mandy asked after they were far enough away.

"Nothing's the matter," I lied. I didn't know what to say to Mandy. I just couldn't put what I was feeling into words. I certainly couldn't tell her what had happened on Friday between Travis and me. For that matter, I didn't even know what had happened between us, or what it meant.

I finally told her the one thing I did know. "I've just got to get Travis on his crutches, that's all. And I've got to do it soon."

Mandy smiled a little, and I could tell she didn't believe what I said. She leaned over the table, close to me. "Darcy, you don't have to tell me what's bothering you. I'll stick with you. You're my friend."

For some strange reason her words choked me up inside, and I began to cry. Why, oh why, were my feelings always getting in the way of just being real with people?

"I've got to see Chip," I said, dabbing my eyes with my crumpled paper napkin. "Take my lunch plate up, will ya?" I shoved away from the table.

"But he's in study hall; you won't be able to see him."

"I'll find a way. I have to talk to him!" I headed toward the door, wiping away more tears with the back of my hand.

The hallways were empty, and I was grateful that no one could see my red eyes. I pulled up outside of

Chip's study hall. The door to the back of the classroom was open, and I wheeled in just far enough to keep the teacher from seeing me. Chip was in the last row, bent over his homework.

I waved to catch the eye of the kid next to him and pointed to Chip. "Get Chip," I mouthed silently.

The boy understood and tapped Chip on the shoulder. He nodded in my direction.

"I need to talk to you," I mouthed when Chip looked my way.

He got up from his desk and walked up the aisle to the teacher. I lost sight of him for a moment, but he soon came out to the hallway with a rest room pass in his hand. "Down this way," he whispered, pointing to the water fountain twenty feet away.

"What's up?" he asked when we arrived.

I wanted desperately to tell him that I was an emotional wreck and that he was part of it and that I needed to see him to tell him the truth. But sitting there next to him, my mouth went dry. My mind raced for words to fill the space between us. Then a thought hit me.

"Listen. You need to come and see Travis today. He's doing a lot better, and I think it's the right time for you to talk to him. He'd like to talk to you."

"You think so?"

"I'm sure of it," I said.

"I'm surprised it's so soon, but you should know best. Thanks, Darcy."

"Why thank me?" I asked with a funny look.

"For doing the advance work—talking with Travis and getting him to warm up to the idea of seeing me. I wouldn't dare go into that hospital if it weren't for you helping out."

My mouth got suddenly drier. I had totally forgotten the promise I had made. What was worse, I had done absolutely no advance work for Chip. But I had made it sound as if I had smoothed the way. Now I was caught in a lie. A serious lie.

Oh, what a mess, Lord. What do I do now? The words from I Corinthians suddenly whispered inside my head. *Love does not get its own way.* At that moment, I should have listened to the words, but I buried them. I just smiled as if Chip were right.

"I can't go this afternoon, though," he said. "How about Friday?"

Why didn't I listen to the voice inside my head? "No, it really has to be today! Late this afternoon . . . like around four-thirty or so. Please?"

Chip didn't know what to say. It was obvious he had plans, but my pleading look and my red eyes forced him into it.

"Okay, I'll be there. Maybe I'll stop by the store and get him something to do while he's in the hospital." Chip was thinking out loud, warming to the idea. His eyes brightened, and he smiled a sincere smile—the smile that had always attracted me to him.

It was then that I understood why I wanted Chip to visit Travis so badly. If Travis got mad at Chip, or if he saw what a nice guy Chip is, his attention would be off me. And maybe, just maybe, if he saw what neat friends Chip and I are, he'd give up the idea of the two of us.

It was a messy plan. And it seemed even messier at four-thirty that afternoon. For one thing, Travis was definitely acting different. He kept smiling at me while he worked on the weights in the PT room. He talked the way a real friend would—not like the dumb boyfriend stuff I pictured.

Why is he doing this? He can't really like me as a friend. Something's weird here.

I distracted his attention away from me. "So, do you want to try the crutches today?"

He dropped his smile and stared into space. "No."

"Why not?"

"Because I don't want to. Just forget about it."

"But—"

His cold stare interrupted me. I looked away, angry with myself for bringing up the subject. He continued his workout as I went to help one of the orderlies put towels away. I watched Travis from a distance. He finished his exercises and wheeled over to me.

"Let's just go to the solarium, okay?" he asked.

Now what? I wondered. I felt sick to my stomach. *What does he want?* I followed him out into the hallway and trailed behind him the whole way to the solarium. When I arrived, he had already parked his chair next to the window.

The scene took my breath away. The room was more beautiful than ever before. The sun was not just orange as it had been last Friday, but was fiery red. The light it cast on everything in the room was too hard to describe. Everything looked as though it could breathe and move. Even the black coffee table seemed to come to life under the sun's rays.

"Just look at that," Travis said to me from his place next to the window. "Come over here and watch the sun go down."

I pulled up next to him. The sun was indeed worth watching. The bottom rim hung just inches over the hills in the distance. It was a perfect circle in the sky, glowing in rich reds and golds.

We stared at it for several minutes. When it was halfway behind the hill, Travis turned to me. "Thanks for making it special," he said.

I gave him a puzzled look.

"The sunset. It's more special with you. And thanks for sticking by me, even when I snapped at you. I know you meant well about trying to get me to walk. I've never had a friend who's stuck by me like you. All the other kids hang around me because I'm on the basketball team or because they think I'm with it."

It was as if the warm glow of the sun had melted my heart, and I found myself drawn to Travis again. *Not again.* What was going on? Just hours earlier I had pinned my heart on Chip. Now it was doing flip-flops. I looked at Travis closer and realized something sobering: he had actually shared his true self with me. With me! He would have never confessed his true colors like this with just anybody.

Confused or not, I now found myself wishing

for a closer friendship with Travis. *He's not a jerk. He does just want me for a friend. Incredible!*

As quickly as this new level of friendship was beginning to take shape, a chilling thought entered my mind. *Chip is coming today!* If there had been time, I would have called Chip at home and told him not to come. But it was too late.

Much too late, in fact. No sooner had I thought of calling him than I heard his voice in the hallway just outside the solarium. Travis and I both turned to face the doorway.

Chip walked slowly into the room, as if he sensed he was intruding.

Travis gave him a look that said "What are you doing here?"

Then Chip gave me a "What's up?" look and tried to smile at Travis. He stumbled to find the right words for what was obviously an awkward encounter. "Uh . . . here." He handed Travis a box. "I thought that you could maybe, you know, hook it up in your room. It's a Nerf basketball set. You, uh . . . you could practice for next year's game."

Chip awkwardly held the box out in mid air, but Travis didn't reach out to take it.

I suddenly felt hot and dizzy, full of guilt and regret. I was too numb to move away from my place next to Travis by the window. Chip stood alone like a puppy who'd just been scolded. He bravely continued.

"Darcy told me you're doing a lot better and that we might be able to talk. What do you think?"

Travis looked at me angrily. Then he shoved his

wheels hard and sped past me and past Chip. "Get out of my face, nerd!" he said to Chip as he almost sideswiped him.

Chip stood there, still holding the gift. He didn't bother to turn around to watch Travis leave. He just stared at me.

I hung my head down. I had no words.

"What's going on?" he asked. "I thought you said I should talk to him. You said he seemed ready."

I looked up at Chip with hollow eyes.

"You didn't talk to him at all, did you?" Chip accused me. "You lied to me!"

His words stung. I hung my head down and started to cry.

"Here. You give it to him." Chip dropped the gift in my lap and walked away.

9

The solarium no longer felt like the friendly, intimate place I had always known it as. The walls lost their burgundy colored warmth as the sun set completely. I shivered at the cold and at my loneliness.

"Why is this happening?" I asked out loud.

The plants and furniture didn't answer. The canary sat still. In my heart I knew the answer, but I was too afraid to admit it. Leaving the solarium, I headed for the fourth floor and an old friend. Maybe Mrs. Hamlin could help me. I only had a few minutes before Monica would come to pick me up, but even a few minutes of comfort from Mrs. Hamlin would ease the pain.

As I wheeled into her room, I saw that she was wearing a skirt and sweater and was packing her suitcase.

"Are you leaving?" I asked without saying hello.

She looked up from the suitcase. "Why, yes, dear. I just got word an hour ago. Isn't that wonderful? The doctor says I'll be better off at home now."

I must have looked disappointed.

"Is that okay with you?" she asked.

"Well, yeah, that's great." I tried to act excited. "It's just that I didn't know. I figured you'd be around a while."

"I thought so, too, but. . . ." She stopped and came around to my side of the bed. "Darcy, is something wrong?"

Her question released all my feelings, and I spilled out everything. I told her exactly what happened and why.

"I care about Chip a lot. But Travis is a really neat guy, and maybe I can help him. Or at least I *could* have helped him. I don't think it's possible now. Oh, I don't know. I just wanted to love everyone."

"Do you really want that, Darcy?" Mrs. Hamlin asked.

I fumbled with Chip's gift that still sat on my lap. "Yeah. Of course. I just don't know how."

Mrs. Hamlin reached to the bottom of her suitcase. "Well, then, let's find out, shall we?" She pulled out her tattered Bible.

"What are you going to do?" I kidded through my tears, "look up 'confused girl caught between two friends' in the concordance?"

"No, but I will show you something this old lady learned a long time ago. Here, you look it up. It's the perfect prescription for you. Philippians 1:9." She handed me the Bible.

I hesitated.

"Go on. Look it up and read it to me."

I began flipping through the now familiar Bible. In the last few weeks, it had become my friend, just as Mrs. Hamlin had. I found Philippians and scanned down the page until my eyes rested on the ninth verse.

I began reading softly. "My prayer for you is that you will overflow more and more with love for others and at the same time keep on growing in spiritual knowledge and insight. For I want you always to see clearly the difference between right and wrong, and to be inwardly clean, no one being able to criticize you."

I felt like the words were written for me, Darcy DeAngelis, a seventh-grade girl from Jordan Junior High. Everything about the verse hit home.

I had let my heart rule the way, with my feelings jerking me all over the place.

I had not seen clearly the difference between right and wrong.

I was not clean on the inside.

There was plenty to criticize about the way I had acted.

Chip had every right to be upset. Travis, too. I hadn't been honest with them.

"But I was being loving, wasn't I?" I asked. "I mean, I did change."

"Yes, dear, of course, but you're still learning. Love doesn't always come automatically. And the things that feel right about love aren't always the right things. Love is blind, the world says. But God wants you to have 20/20 vision when it comes to love. Too many people try to love others without God."

"Like the way I tried to love Travis?"

"That's right. But God wants you to understand things from His point of view." She pointed to her head with her crooked finger. "It means letting your heart listen to your head, and letting your head listen to God."

My heart needs to listen to my head, and my head needs to listen to God. Wow. I closed the Bible and placed it on her bed. Mrs. Hamlin's words—God's words—explained everything. I felt bad for what I'd done, but I was glad that my heart and head were beginning to get straightened out. I was also glad that I was forgiven.

"Thanks Mrs. Hamlin. I'm going to remember you forever."

"Nonsense. You'll forget me soon."

"No, I won't!" I protested.

"Oh, I don't mean you'll forget my name or face. But many people like me will come and go in your life. All I ask you to remember about me is our time together and my Bible."

I hugged her tightly. She returned a warm grandmalike hug and kiss on my cheek.

"Now get on with you," she said. "Your mother will be here soon, I imagine."

"No, my sister, Monica, is picking me up."

"That's right!" came a voice from behind. It was Monica, standing with her hands on her hips in the hallway. "And you're late!"

"Oops, I did it again." I laughed as I turned away from Mrs. Hamlin. "See ya."

Monica just shook her head and complained about my forgetfulness all the way to the elevator. I listened without snapping back. I was busy planning my next steps to do what was right. When we arrived at the elevator, I pressed the button and turned to Monica. "I love you, too, sis. I'm sorry I was late. I'll do better next time."

She frowned, surprised that I'd so easily confess my error. "Good. Just don't forget it when next time comes. By the way, we're stopping for Chinese food."

"Yesss!" I clenched my fist in victory. There's nothing like Chinese food after a good cry.

My hopes of doing the right thing didn't go very well the next day. Chip and his family got word that his grandmother in Nebraska had passed away, and he had to fly out for the funeral. He wouldn't be back till Thursday or Friday. I was dying to apologize to him face-to-face, but it would have to wait.

My next step was to try and help Travis the best I could. During our time in physical therapy I explained why Chip had come to visit. I didn't leave anything out and was surprised, when I finished, how clean I felt on the inside. Travis seemed to understand, though he was still angry with Chip.

"Who does he think he is, anyway?" Travis asked. "I bet he thinks he's better than me. Doesn't he realize what he did? I may never walk again!"

I didn't argue with Travis about Chip. I did

argue about his not walking again.

"Listen, Travis. You can't talk that way! You *will* walk again! The doctors—"

"The doctors don't know what it feels like!" He wheeled his way to the elevators.

"But I know you can do it. I believe in you," I said, a few steps behind him. Then I remembered the part from I Corinthians 13. *You will always believe in him and always expect the best in him.* "I really care about you, Travis. You're my friend."

Travis stopped and turned sharply around. He was angrier still.

"What is this about?! Have you just been helping me because you want to go out with me or something?"

"No, you don't understand! I'm not talking about some romantic-type stuff. I mean I care about you. I really care. That's what love is. Let me show you something." Without stopping to feel embarrassed or self-conscious, I reached into my backpack and pulled out my Bible.

"It says here, 'If you love someone, you will be loyal to him no matter what the cost. You will always believe in him, always expect the best in him.' Travis, that's what friends are for. I'm just trying to help you."

Travis looked puzzled. "So you don't want to go out with me?"

"Travis," I said, "I think you're a nice guy. And like all the girls say, you're really cute. But do you remember what you said in the solarium about my being your friend? Well, that's what I'm saying, too.

That's what God calls love."

"Well, I don't believe everything in the Bible, but if it says stuff like that, it can't be all bad, I guess. And I suppose I understand. You're right. I'm sorry I got mad."

"And I'm sorry I forced Chip on you."

"Yeah . . . your friend." He gave a little sneer.

I smiled confidently. "Yeah, my friend!" I said with pride. "And you, too, okay?"

"Yeah, friends."

"Good, now I can bug you about walking."

"Aaugh," Travis groaned.

I couldn't convince him to stand up on his crutches, but at least he laughed about it rather than ignoring or dropping it. I was making progress.

I spent the rest of the week going through my normal routines at school and at the hospital. Homeroom, classes, locker, lunch, classes, pickup at the curb side, and then on to candy striping. I worked hard with Travis trying to get him to use his crutches, but with no success. His stubbornness tested my resolve to love him and help him to be his best.

It wasn't until Friday that my creative juices really got going. The night before Travis had called to report that his doctor said he could go home and that he could return to school on Monday.

I went to work right away on Friday morning. In the lobby as the kids were coming into school, I flagged down every cheerleader I knew. They looked at me kind of weird, but they also knew I had a special "in" with their number-one man. I had them circle around my wheelchair and then I explained.

"Listen, guys," I said. "Travis is coming back on Monday."

"Oooh, awesome!" one said.

"Yeah. Awesome. But listen, we've got to make it a real special day. I want to plan a welcome at the entrance of school on Monday morning. We'll get everyone out there and make a big deal of it."

"Like, of course. But what do you want us to like, you know, do? Just stand out there?" one asked, chewing her gum and flipping her hair behind her shoulders.

I resisted the temptation to make fun. Instead, I carefully explained what they needed to do. "Wear your uniforms. And bring pompons. Jump up and down and do your normal stuff like, 'Travis, Travis, he's our man . . .' Got it?"

"No problem," one of them said.

"Good idea, kid," said another as she bounced away with her girlfriend. "We'll be there, for sure. And, hey! You're not such a nerd after all."

"Thanks . . . I think," I answered with a smile. I was feeling too good to be bothered by the comment.

I looked at my watch. Ten minutes till homeroom. That gave me enough time to head down to the art class. When I explained that Travis was coming back on Monday, Mrs. Juarez was eager to help with the welcome too.

"I'll have the seventh-period class make the

poster, Darcy. About eight feet wide, will that do?"

"Sure thing. Have it say something like, 'Welcome Back, Hero!' "

"Okay. We'll handle it. Oh, and what time should we have it out there?"

"I figure I can ask Mrs. McAllister to bring Travis a little before homeroom starts. So if we're out there around ten after eight, it will be perfect. We'll all meet in the lobby and then fling open the doors to surprise Travis when he comes."

Mrs. Juarez was really getting caught up in the whole thing, but then she got a serious look on her face. "Is this okay with the administration? Have you checked with Mr. Sandstrom?"

"I was just on my way there. If he says no, I'll tell you. Otherwise plan on the poster."

Mr. Sandstrom thought it was a great idea. He even volunteered to give a speech, but I thought just a handshake would do.

By the time school was out, everyone was talking about the welcome back. The only thing left to do was talk with Chip. I knew he would be returning late that night from Nebraska . . . too late for me to go over his house or even call. I would have to talk to him Sunday at church.

With a quick call to Chip's house on Saturday morning, I set up a time we could meet before Sunday school. He didn't sound particularly thrilled, and I couldn't blame him. I spent all day Saturday wishing that time would fly faster.

Finally, Sunday dawned and I found myself alone

with Chip in an empty classroom. My stomach was tied up in knots, and my hands felt cold and sweaty. Chip sat in a chair two rows away from me. He glanced at me and then looked all around the room. Not finding anything of interest, he began examining the sole of his sneaker. He rubbed at the sole, as if trying to erase something. He looked as nervous as I felt.

"Did you hear about the welcome we're planning for Travis?" I asked as a way of breaking the ice.

"You mean that *you've* planned," he said sarcastically. He still wouldn't look at me.

I was itching to shoot back something smart, but I remembered why I was there. "Yes, the welcome back I've planned."

"Why are you doing it? Is this a way for you to get even closer to Travis?"

"No!" I protested. I sensed Chip's jealousy and didn't feel so upset. "That's not it at all. Don't you realize this is only to help Travis? He honestly doesn't think he'll walk again. He needs everyone's encouragement. I'm not doing this so Travis will like me, Chip. I'm just trying to be a friend. I'm trying to love him the way Jesus would."

It was easy saying Jesus' name in a Sunday school classroom. But it was the truth.

"Chip, you're still my friend. I know I didn't treat you like a friend. I lied to you about Travis. That was wrong, and I'm really sorry." I chose my next words carefully. "I care about you a lot. You're special to me."

To my disappointment, Chip showed no emotion. But at last he mumbled, "I forgive you."

"Will you be there with me on Monday to welcome Travis?"

"Yeah. I'll be there. But maybe Travis doesn't want to see me there. Won't I spoil it for everyone?"

"You need to be there, Chip. Please trust me. And, Chip?"

"Yeah?"

"Stick by me, okay?"

10

Monday morning was all I had hoped it would be. The entire school was there, waiting to give Travis a rousing welcome. Word had spread like wildfire, and kids had to line up around the drive-up circle as well as pack the lobby, there were so many.

The band was out in full uniform. The banner that the art class made was spectacular. They had used sparkles, streamers, and every color imaginable. The cheerleaders were decked out and shaking their pompons as if this were the championship game.

"You ought to be a campaign manager for the next president, Darcy," Mr. Sandstrom commented.

I felt proud. This was going to be a biggie!

I was parked in my chair just inside the lobby. I had dressed nicely for the occasion, and EJ stood next to me with a red bow tied to his collar. His whole body wagged because of all the noise and excitement. Mandy, April, and Kendra were lined up to my left. Chip stood behind EJ with his hands in his pockets, obviously uncomfortable.

Soon Mrs. McAllister drove into the circle. The McAllisters' car was long and fancy, almost like a limousine. Travis's mom got out and walked around to the back, smiling nervously. Two teachers stepped forward to offer a hand as she opened the trunk to get the wheelchair out.

Travis opened his door and swung around, sitting on the edge of the seat. He moved easily into the wheelchair by himself. He had learned a lot about using a chair. I was disappointed that he wasn't walking, but I was prepared. My full plan was yet to unfold.

The kids all yelled out greetings and cat-calls and whistles. Travis looked around at everyone and smiled. He raised a fist in triumph when the band struck up the school fight song, and a roaring cheer went up from the crowd.

Mrs. McAllister started to push Travis up the ramp, but he shooed her away and began wheeling himself. The cheerleaders, their bare legs looking blue from standing out in the cold, moved in a giggling mass toward Travis. One girl grabbed his books off his lap and another managed to give Travis a kiss.

The band was on the second verse of the school song by the time Travis came through the front door of the lobby. Cymbals clashed and we all moved forward to officially greet the returning hero. Mr. Sandstrom extended his hand for a welcoming handshake. A couple of cameras flashed.

Confetti covered everything.

EJ and I moved directly in front of Travis as Mr. Sandstrom stepped aside.

"Welcome back," I said with a smile.

"Thanks," Travis responded, still looking around him and acknowledging those cheering him on. "Yo, big Boo-Bah!" he hoarsely called to a fellow basketball player who was throwing wads of crepe paper at Travis's wheels. He grinned at a couple others and gave thumbs-up to a few of his friends from his homeroom.

"Travis," I said loudly to catch his attention.

"Heads up, everybody," Travis shouted. "The kid here has something to say." He looked at me with a grown-up smile, and everyone quieted down.

"Travis, I want to give you something. Chip?" I said, looking over my shoulder. "Can you bring them here?"

Chip stepped forward from behind EJ, holding a pair of crutches. He placed them across my lap.

"These are for you," I said to Travis, holding the crutches out at arm's length. It looked as if I were presenting him a trophy. Or maybe a dare.

He glared at me. The smile drained from his face, and his neck muscles got tight.

"Go ahead. Take 'em," I said not quite as loudly.

Travis tried to wheel around me on my right side, but EJ pulled me to the side and blocked the way. Travis's eyes narrowed. I was like a basketball player blocking his path to the basket.

"Go on, take 'em. You're back now. You can do it."

The crowd began to urge Travis on with nods and chanting. "C'mon, Travis. Go Travis."

He looked around, trying to hide his bewilderment. Travis knew he was trapped and slowly reached for the crutches. For an instant, both our hands held onto the crutches, and I could feel him shaking. He jerked them out of my grasp, and I backed up to give him room. His mother locked the wheels of his wheelchair as he slid forward. He then placed both crutches in front of him. With one last look at me, he slowly, very slowly, pulled himself up. He rocked back and forth for several seconds before steadying himself. Then he raised his head and gritted his teeth in a tight grin. I couldn't tell if it was from victory or from pain.

An explosive cheer went up all around us. "All right! Go get 'em, Travis. Way to go!"

"You did it!" I said, clapping and smiling. "I knew you could."

I had daydreamed about the different things that might happen next. Would he bend down and hug me? Would he and Chip shake hands? Would we go down the hallway to our lockers together? Would he say thanks?

What occurred next happened so quickly and quietly, no one noticed but me. It wasn't anything Travis said. It was the way he walked by me. I saw it as if it were in slow motion. Travis blinked his eyes and then walked ahead without looking down at me or waiting for me to join him.

It was as if the act of standing on his own and leaving the wheelchair behind also meant he was leaving behind everything about the last few weeks. He walked by me as he had walked by a hundred other admiring seventh graders who wished they were his friend.

It was as if I were not there. As if I had not pushed him to accept the challenge of walking. As if I had not planned the welcoming party. As if I had not coached him all those weeks in PT. As if we had never shared golden sunsets. As if he had never kissed me.

No one else noticed it. A mass of kids moved together down the hall, following Travis. A few cheers echoed as he walked through the hall to his locker.

No one noticed, that is, except Chip.

Chip stood next to me. We watched everyone leave the lobby until we were the last ones there, except for a few art students who were rolling up the banner to carry it back to class. Crepe paper and pieces of the cheerleaders' pompons lay on the floor. The sound of the band could be heard in the distance as it played its way back to the music room. Finally, the lobby was quiet and empty. It seemed a long time before either of us spoke.

"You did it," Chip finally said.

I didn't turn to look at him. I was still staring down the hall.

"Did what?" I asked at last.

"Got him to walk. That's why you did all this, isn't it?" Chip asked.

"Yes," I confessed.

"You knew what you were doing. You knew you

had to get him to walk. And you knew that guys like Travis live for the crowd. You gave him a chance to be a hero in front of everyone." Chip stood in front of me. "And one other thing. You knew he'd ignore you, didn't you?"

I was on the verge of crying. "I . . . I don't know. Maybe I did."

"Then why? Why did you do it?"

"Because I had to." All that Mrs. Hamlin taught me flooded my memory again. "Because love . . . real love . . . does that. It lets the truth win out. It hopes for and seeks the best in someone else. If I really loved him, I had to do it. Even if it meant I'd lose him as a friend."

"I Corinthians 13?" Chip asked.

"Uh, huh."

"Show it to me, Darcy."

I reached behind me and took out my Bible. I opened it to the now familiar passage. Chip took it from my hands and began to read.

"If you love someone, you will be loyal to him, no matter what the cost. You will always believe in him and always expect the best of him."

I smiled as he read it. I realized just how much I cared about Chip. I wanted to stick by him. And expect the best of him.

Chip reached into his pocket and pulled out a pen. He marked something in my Bible and then laid it on my lap. There in the margin next to the thirteenth chapter was a blue heart.

"What did you do that for?" I asked.

"Tomorrow's Valentine's Day, remember?"

I blushed, hardly knowing what to say. "Thanks," I murmured.

"For what?"

"For sticking by me. For being here today. For always being there."

"Sure. Always."

He took hold of the handles of my wheelchair. "Move over, EJ. Today your owner is a hero, so I get to help her to class."

EJ barked as if he understood. We headed down the hall together as the late bell rang for class. We had learned a lesson before school had even started.

Darcy

"Let's have a Feel-Sorry-for-Darcy Day."

That's what Darcy's sister says when Darcy sulks over having to stay with her parents at family camp, instead of rooming with the other girls her age. Once more, her wheelchair has set her apart.

Darcy is tired of being different. Tired of putting up a good front. Tired of putting up with insensitive remarks. Tired of being left out. But her time at camp brings some surprises, and Darcy learns more than she could have imagined about prayer, about God, about her friends . . . and about herself.

JONI EARECKSON TADA has been in a wheelchair herself since she was seventeen. Her story has been told in the books Joni and Choices/Changes and the film Joni. The Christian Fund for the Disabled, an organization that Joni started, works to bring together disabled people and caring churches.

Chariot Books™
A Division of Cook Communications

Darcy and the Meanest Teacher in the World

"Don't be silly, Darcy. I suggest you find more suitable activities."

Mrs. Crowhurst's abrupt putdown in front of a gymfull of seventh graders leaves Darcy angry and humiliated. It isn't that Darcy cares so deeply about being manager of the girls' basketball team—it's just that "The Crow" seems to have it in for her.

Darcy decides to do some investigative journalism for the school paper on the topic of mean teachers. She's sure that her "expose" will win her the respect and admiration of her peers—not to mention their votes when she runs for president of the student government.

But why aren't her faithful sidekicks, Mandy and Chip, very enthusiastic about her project? And why doesn't she want her parents or journalism advisor to know what she's up to?

JONI EARECKSON TADA has been in a wheelchair herself since she was seventeen. Her story has been told in the books *Joni* and *Choices/Changes* and the film *Joni*.

Chariot Books™
A Division of Cook Communications

Meet My Friends

Three stories of ordinary kids … with EXTRAordinary courage.

Have you ever wondered what life would be like if you couldn't see? or hear? or walk? Aimee, Jamie, and Josh can tell you.

Except for their disabilities, they're pretty ordinary kids. They enjoy sports, talk to God, have pets, fight with little brothers, and want to be liked by their classmates at school. In fact, they're a lot like you.

Their stories are told by JONI EARECKSON TADA, who's been in a wheelchair herself since she was seventeen. Since then, God has taken Joni on some great adventures. She's met a lot of grown-ups and kids with different kinds of disabilities. And she's found that behind the handicaps are real, ordinary people with real, ordinary hopes and fears and dreams . . . and a lot of courage.

Come along with Joni . . . and meet her friends!

Chariot Books
A Division of Cook Communications

❖ PARENTS ❖

Are you looking for fun ways to bring the Bible to life in the lives of your children?

Chariot Family Publishing has hundreds of books, toys, games, and videos that help teach your children the Bible and apply it to their everyday lives.

Look for these educational, inspirational, and fun products at your local Christian bookstore.